I0781258

Her Wicked Knight

JEN BRADLEE

Her Wicked Knight

Copyright © 2023 Kirsten S. Blacketer/Jen Bradlee.

All rights reserved. This book or any portion thereof may not be reproduced or used in any manner whatsoever without the express written permission of the publisher except for the use of brief quotations in a book review.

This is a work of fiction. Similarities to real people, places, or events are entirely coincidental.

Printed in the United States of America.
First Printing, 2023
ISBN: 978-1966905134

Cover Art by The Midnight Muse
Written by Jen Bradlee
Published by BlackShip Press
Kirsten.blacketer@gmail.com
https://kirstensblacketer.com/jen-bradlee/

Dedication

To the other *Guy and Marian* who inspired this story.

I blame you, Richard Armitage. No one should look that good in guyliner.

A Letter from the Author

Dear Reader,

Welcome and thank you for selecting *Her Wicked Knight* for your reading pleasure. I truly hope you enjoy the story and fall in love with Guy and Marian.

Allow me to preface with a warning. If you're not a fan of anti-heroes with dominating and questionable morals, explicit intimate scenes, or graphic language and violence, then this may not be the book for you. For a complete list of content forewarnings, please visit kirstensblacketer.com/jen-bradlee.

If that's exactly what you're looking for, then allow me to welcome you and proceed.

Sending warm regards and best wishes your way. Remember to be kind and love one another.

Sincerely,

Jen Bradlee

Table of Contents

Chapter One

London, England 1415

Mistress Marian Ravenwood of Ravinell would much rather dine with her father's hogs than beg for an audience with King Henry V and suffer the pomposity of those around him. She preferred the animals' poor manners and honest stench to the company of the lords and ladies of the royal court.

And yet, duty demanded sacrifice. With a false smile pasted on her lips, she greeted everyone with measured civility. So long as she remained in motion, none could corner her with false sentiments of concern for her father's health or to question the stability of his lands.

There was not one soul among them she could trust. Not even King Henry.

"Have you seen him?" One lady whispered behind her, dramatically adding, "The Grim Knight?"

"Saints. Is he here?" another replied, her voice low.

Marian gritted her teeth, eager to be away from the gossip. She cared little for courtly games or incessant murmurs. The whispers sounded like ravens feasting on rotting flesh.

"Rumor has it, the king granted him a holding in the north for his service to the crown." Another whisper brushed her.

"The Grim Knight," a breathy sigh echoed. "I have heard tell he is as handsome as he is bloodthirsty."

"They say he has slaughtered thousands," yet another lady said, her voice drowning in mock horror. "Bathing in the blood of innocents. Slaughtering men in his path. Raping women before slitting their throats. Pillaging enemy villages, selling children to slavers."

The whispering women gasped.

Marian scoffed at the outlandish tales, moving to a quiet

place to await her audience with the king, her stomach already twisted in knots at the thought of revealing her desperation. With so many eager to gossip, she wondered at the wisdom of her request for aid during such a spectacle.

'Twas little wonder the kingdom struggled under the yoke of adversity. The court cared nothing for what was beyond the walls of their protected holdings, even while basking in the misfortune of others. Trapped in such garish flamboyancy, Marian was left with no illusion as to the nobility's true nature. They cared only for themselves and their pockets. None here knew the value of an honest day's labor or the gnawing hunger of an empty larder.

The king would hear her plea for aid, then she would return home. It was the sole reason for this arduous journey from Cumberland to London. After her father had become ill, many of the baron's responsibilities had fallen upon her shoulders, as she was the only child of the Baron Ravinell. She had risen to the occasion and followed her father's instructions, ensuring they were carried out to the letter.

Then the raids increased from one or two a year to the same number in a month. Her lands, her people were suffering from the actions of those who raped and pillaged the villages along the border. Naught could be done but to petition the king to seek out the raiders and end their ruthless attacks on his subjects.

"Mistress Marian." A familiar voice drifted to her through the sea of courtiers.

Marian turned to find Lord Graham de Bough, baron of a neighboring estate to her father's, a goblet in hand, eyeing her with amusement.

"My lord." She bobbed a curtsy.

"Well, is this not a pleasant surprise?" He smiled with easy charm. "Had I known you were coming to London, I would have offered to personally escort you."

"You are too kind, my lord." Unease settled over Marian as curious gazes fell upon them. She'd known Graham since they were children, and she was loath to give the court any morsel to gnaw upon.

"How is your father?" Graham's concern melted her reservations. "I take it he is too unwell to travel, as you are here in his stead."

"On the contrary. Father is doing well, but such a tiresome journey could cause him to relapse into an unfit state." The lie slipped easily from her tongue. "I offered to come in his stead."

A glimmering ray of sunlight from a nearby window struck Graham, illuminating his golden hair and radiant blue eyes, bluer than the sky stretching overhead in the summer. He smiled. "Of course."

"What brings you to London, my lord?" Marian smoothed the soft fabric of her skirts. Her nerves twisted into a knotted ball of yarn in the pit of her stomach.

"I had some business matters."

"But why are you *here*?" she whispered conspiratorially.

His knowing smile eased her fluttering nerves. "I have come purely for the entertainment of watching them all grovel for favor."

"You take enjoyment in their discomfort?"

He lifted his shoulder in a noncommittal fashion. The rich vibrant fabrics he wore merged perfectly with the opulence around them…and yet, for all his ability to blend in with this world, he stood apart. Whether it was his handsome gilded appearance or his smoldering charm, she could not be certain. One thing Marian knew, when she stood thus, speaking with him, she almost felt the comfort of home. *Almost.*

The reminder of home and the problems that awaited her there sobered her instantly.

"Why have you come to London, my lady?"

His question lingered for several heartbeats.

"The…incidents on our land have increased. Our tenants can no longer bear the strain and ask for protection from the ongoing raids." Marian folded her hands together and met his concerned gaze.

"They *are* becoming more of a problem." He pondered for a moment. "Have you brought this to the attention of Lord Hayworth, your neighbor to the west?"

"I have. He has not offered much in the way of support or solution." Marian sighed in exasperation. "There is nothing I can do now but petition the king for aid."

"If we join forces, we could create something to be reckoned with." His eyes sparkled. "Our marriage would combine two powerful families. No one would dare cross us. The raids would end. Peace and prosperity would reign."

Marian's face warmed at his offhand proposal. "Your offer is gracious, my lord, but I am unconvinced our union would be enough to bring an end to the terror and bloodshed."

"Perha—" Graham's reply died abruptly as the air in the room shifted.

A darkness permeated the glittering gathering. Marian turned toward the entrance, where a tall man, clad in black leather, stepped into the throng of courtiers. His dark head towered above the rest, moving through the crowd, a grim specter gliding through a field of roses.

Marian gasped as his attention drifted across her. His dark, haunting eyes lingered on her for several breaths before he pivoted away.

"Is something wrong, my lady?" Graham asked.

"All is well." She pressed a hand to her bodice and smiled. "If you will excuse me, I must prepare for my audience with the king."

"Of course. If you require my services, please do not hesitate to ask. I am your humble servant."

His bow left her warm and uncertain. Why couldn't she just accept his suit and solve her problems without involving the king or his court?

Because you do not love him. Marian scoffed at the small voice in her mind. *Love.* What was love but a novelty? A wish. A dream. Fanciful and wonderful, but unrealistic. Her dreams of love had died when she was young, when she realized how the world truly worked and what value her life truly held.

Love would not protect her people. Love would not return her father's health.

She crossed the room, weaving through courtiers. She

needed to speak with the king and leave as quickly as possible. Another moment trapped in this room and she would go mad.

As she rounded the corner, Marian collided with a wall. She steadied herself, pressing her hand against it. Warmth infused her fingertips.

She jerked her hand away from…not a wall but the firm chest of the dark interloper. Instead of offering an apology, he glowered at her.

"I beg your pardon." Marian huffed at his lapse in manners but managed to—barely—keep hold of her own.

"You should be aware of your surroundings."

The timbre of his voice left her breathless. Deep as a fathomless pit, it shook her senses.

The words formed meaning in her mind.

"How dare you insinuate I am unaware of my surroundings." Marian took stock of their position. They were at the edge of the crowd, tucked in a small alcove along the side of the room. "It is you who lurks in shadows, waiting to prey on the unsuspecting."

He scoffed. "If it takes so little to unsettle you, I wonder at your ability to survive this cruel world."

Marian snapped her mouth closed. He had a point, but she would not give him satisfaction by acknowledging it. She studied him for a long moment, taking full measure of the man before her.

Tall as an oak and nearly as broad, he wore not a stitch of color. Clothed in black from head to toe, he left an intimidating impression. Upon closer inspection, she noted his eyes—framed by impossibly thick lashes—were not black as she'd previously thought, but a deep amber with dark green woven through like an embroidered tapestry. Black waves of thick hair fell around his face.

Saints, but he was striking.

"Your name, sir, so I might notify the king of such an impudent cur at his court?"

A deep chuckle escaped him, the sound striking her with the force of an arrow piercing its target. Curse him.

"The king knows of my exploits and…personal proclivities." His lips curled into a sneer. "And he not only celebrates them but handsomely rewards them."

"A man of your position should help those in need not lord his status over those he deems less worthy." Marian matched his stance, tilting her head to hold his intense gaze.

"And what of your name? It seems you have lost your manners as well." His sneer transformed to a feral grin. "Or shall I give you a name suited to a beastie of your temperament?"

"You, sir, have proven yourself unworthy of the honor of my company. I would rather gnaw off my arm than hear my name from your foul lips."

"His Majesty, King Henry V." An attendant announced the king's arrival above the rippling conversation of the crowd.

As the room fell to order, Marian took one final look at the black-clad bastard before spinning on her heel, away from his brooding glare. Turning her back to him might have been unwise, but it left her with lingering satisfaction.

She took her place with the other courtiers awaiting their opportunity to petition the king. Her heart thundered in her chest as the room settled into silence when the king appeared.

Everyone bowed low and waited patiently.

When her name was called, she approached the king with humility and grace. Curtsying low, she waited for him to speak.

The attendant introduced her. "Marian Ravenwood, daughter of Jonas Ravenwood, Baron Ravinell, Your Majesty."

"Rise," King Henry said with a wave of his hand. "Proceed."

Unable to focus on anything but her plea, Marian explained the dire situation in which her people found themselves with the same passion as when she spoke with Graham. She highlighted the necessity of maintaining law and order to quell the increasing violence on the border with Scotland.

"What would you have me do?"

"My liege, I beg of you, send a garrison of soldiers to ferret out the raiders and to protect your loyal subjects from these atrocities." Marian bowed her head.

The king pondered her words. After a few moments, he summoned his attendant. Their whispers left the courtiers in strained silence. A cough echoed through the room. When the king straightened, Marian held her breath.

"Your pleas have been heard, Mistress Ravenwood." King Henry inclined his head. "I shall provide a small band of soldiers to aid you."

Relief nearly pulled her to the ground. "May God grant you mercy, Your Majesty."

"To guarantee these brigands are brought to justice and to ensure efficient results, I shall send my most valued knight."

Marian rose to her full height. "Your most valued knight, Your Majesty?"

"Aye." The king stood, and his voice echoed through the room. "Sir Guy Silverthorne, step forward."

The crowd murmured with excitement as they parted to reveal the one man Marian hoped never to see again, the tall, black-clad bastard who had dared to challenge her. His eyes danced with malevolent merriment when they fixed on her. Damn him.

Sir Guy Silverthorne came beside her and bowed. "I am your humble servant, my liege."

The heat of him surrounded her at his proximity. She loathed being this close to him. How could she possibly reject the generosity of the king by begging for another knight—*any* other knight—to accompany the garrison? The thought of sharing her home, her companionship, with this man for any length of time left her ill.

With a wave of his hand, the king dismissed them both.

Marian ignored the curious courtiers as she took her leave. She cared not whether the horrible black knight followed. This battle would have a new enemy, and not the one she'd intended.

When she thought of the journey home in his company, her mood worsened. Perhaps she should have considered Graham's proposal more seriously. His company was certainly more enjoyable.

Curse them all.

Chapter Two

Nothing had prepared him for the temptation of Mistress Marian Ravenwood.

During all of his exploits, through all of his travels, Guy had never encountered a woman who could infuriate and arouse him in equal measure. The king's command could have been a curse upon his good fortune, but with its promise of more time in the company of the fiery maiden, he embraced the opportunity. It was not as though he had something else to occupy his time. He would relish the challenge she provided.

In the little conversation they'd shared, he found a spark of intelligence and wit to be a bonus to her beauty. The moment he walked into the room, she shone with a brilliance that surpassed every courtier. Even her simple but elegant gown and modest headdress detracted little from the natural glow of her presence. Confidence radiated in her carriage and gentle demeanor.

Until she encountered him.

'Twas then his interest jolted to life with the force of a lightning bolt. His indifference was merely a tool to lure her true nature to the surface, to gain both her disdain and to imprint a lasting memory of him upon her. Judging by her constant glares every time they occupied a room together, his plan had worked.

A fortnight of travel lay before them. What secrets surrounding this delightfully challenging creature would he discover?

Burdened with a garrison of twenty soldiers on horseback, several carts of supplies, and Mistress Marian's entourage, they left London, forging north to Cumberland. Despite the tedious journey, he enjoyed the change of scenery as they ventured toward the border.

Guy took the lead, confident in his ability to make this trip as uncomplicated as possible. Mistress Marian's traveling companions had chosen to travel by horseback, as did she.

A sennight passed, and they progressed northward without incident. They encountered neither brigands nor delays. Guy should have taken the week as a gift, but his experience had taught him not to fall into a comfortable rhythm when a simple misstep could lead to disaster.

The sun hung low on the horizon, but only half a league would have them at a respectable inn with decent meals and comfortable beds, the anticipation of which kept him moving.

The strike of hooves on solid ground alerted him to the presence of a blood bay gelding falling into step beside his black destrier. He did not need to turn to know who sat astride the lovely beast.

"May I inquire as to why we have taken this path?"

"You may, but it does not guarantee I will supply a satisfactory answer."

Her hands tightened on the reins. "If we are to be traveling companions, I require understanding the reason for your apparent detour."

"'Tis not a detour." He looked at her from the corner of his eye.

"The road leading north is behind us." She scowled. "Why do we travel west?"

With a grunt, he turned to her. "I intend to indulge in a hearty meal, a few mugs of ale, perhaps a lusty wench or two, and then avail myself of a bed for the night."

She stared at him. Outrage made her eye twitch.

He delighted to see her so unsettled at his admission. Before she could open her mouth, they crested a hill to see a moderately sized inn tucked into the valley below.

"My refuge awaits." He reined his horse around and sought the captain of the garrison. The men could make camp behind the inn while he found comfort inside.

Many years had he spent lying upon cold, hard ground. Not merely as a page or a knight in training, or even as a soldier readying himself before a battle. Such inconveniences were merely penance for his sins. He had served his time and would no longer deny himself the luxuries he'd worked so diligently toward.

Once the men had their instructions, he urged his horse into a canter down the gentle slope to the inn. There should be room for him…and the lady, should she choose to embrace her station and its benefits.

As he approached the inn, a blur of red flashed by him. Mistress Marian's steed flew with nimble purpose, causing his destrier to snort and sidestep. He shook his head at her impetuousness.

Aye, his quest would prove to be a challenge.

By the time he reached the inn, she had already entered the establishment. He dismounted and handed the reins to a waiting stable boy. With a coin, he ensured the lad would take care of both horses.

The scent of roasted meat mixed with stale ale surrounded him as he entered the building. It took a moment to find her where she blended into shadows along the far wall. Her animated discussion with a small, round woman continued as he approached.

The older woman turned a curious eye to him.

"I require a room, a drink, and a hot meal."

"This fine lady has taken the last of my rooms." The woman sputtered at his scowl. "B-but I will get you the finest meal to be had." She bustled away, looking over her shoulder to be assured he would not drive a dagger into her back.

Guy turned to Mistress Marian, his irritation boiling to the surface. The corners of her mouth turned up in a proud smile.

"Methinks you purchased the last room purely to spite me."

"Perhaps I did. If you will pardon me." She pushed past him.

His hand darted out, taking hold of her wrist, bringing her to an abrupt halt.

Her eyes flared wide. "Unhand me."

"Do not tempt my patience, vixen." He pulled her close until the scent of her teased the edge of his patience. "I have half a mind to drag you to the room you stole from me and force you to share the bed."

A soft gasp ripped from her throat. "You would not dare. A knight would never—"

"Ah…you assume because I am a knight, I follow a code of chivalry and honor." He cupped her chin in his hand. "What surprises I have in store for you, sweeting."

"You are a vile degenerate." She tore herself from him. "I would rather sleep with animals in the barn than share a bed with you."

"By your own assessment, I am nothing more than a wild animal. Would that make my company more bearable?" Delight suffused him at the tension building between them.

Mistress Marian scoffed, turning her gaze to the door.

A drunkard swayed close and brushed against him. He felt the gentle shift of fabric as the thief's nimble fingers attempted to alleviate him of his coin. Guy spun and grabbed the man by the throat.

The thief, covered in filthy garments, gasped as Guy tightened his hold and backed him to the wall. He clawed at Guy's gloved grip and coughed, attempting to free himself, to breathe.

"Release him!" Mistress Marian's command shook the room. Every eye turned to her as she stood beside Guy.

"This thief must learn a lesson." Guy reached into his cloak and removed a small dagger from his hip. When he pressed it to the man's throat, he inhaled deeply, smelling fear permeate the room as every soul took stock and measure of this interaction.

"Will you kill him for stealing?" She attempted to remove his grip, throwing up her hands when he did not yield.

"Aye," Guy hissed, his mind conjuring memories of similar encounters that ended with blood covering his hands. "I have killed for less."

Mistress Marian sucked in a breath. "If you kill him here, now, we will have no recourse but to move on immediately."

She had a point, and he growled in frustration at the thought of a hearty meal and ale. If he followed through with this threat, they would be forced to leave. The garrison would not complain, but Mistress Marian would certainly hold him in contempt.

"Leave," he ordered before dropping the thief and sheathing his dagger.

The man stumbled to the ground and doubled over in a fit of coughing. He eventually righted himself, rubbing his neck, and with a glare in Guy's direction, the man darted to the door.

The assembly returned their attention to their food and drink as he scanned the room. His presence had certainly caused a commotion. *Good.* Now everyone understood he was not to be trifled with.

As he pulled off his cloak, the woman appeared with ale.

"Here are your drinks." She placed two mugs on a nearby table. "I shall fetch your supper directly."

Running his hand through his hair, Guy sat down and picked up a tankard. He saluted the tempting, irate maiden glaring at him.

"Sit." He took a drink. When she did not move, he grabbed her by the skirt and tugged her to the chair beside him.

Spine straight, she pulled the fabric from his grip. "I do not take orders from you."

"Something tells me you take orders from no one." He took another deep drink and watched her over the rim of his cup.

Her shoulders relaxed as she reached for the second tankard.

He admired the way her hand wrapped around the handle, the soft curve of her neck as she lifted the mug to her lips. She wore a simple headdress, but it left little to the imagination as it revealed thick curls beneath it.

As she drank, his body tensed.

How could this woman torment him with so little effort? The scent of rosewater wrapped around him. If he buried his face in her hair, would she smell as sweet as a field of wildflowers in summer?

The old woman reappeared, bearing two bowls of thick, meaty stew and a loaf of dark bread. He nodded in appreciation and reached for the bread after she set it on the table between them.

With gusto, he tore off a piece and scooped stew into his mouth. This would sate his hunger. At least in part. He glimpsed a guarded look on her lovely face as she reached for the bread.

"Savage," she hissed in disgust.

"You say that as though I should be ashamed," he said between bites.

"Aye, you should be." She took a tentative nibble. Her hesitation transformed to large mouthfuls, and she devoured the stew.

"Why?"

"You are a knight of the realm. There are expectations placed upon you for proper conduct and manners, yet you defy them with threats and selfish demands."

He shrugged. "I am not a good and proper man, nor have I ever claimed to be."

Mistress Marian snorted in a most unladylike manner. "Anyone with or without eyes can see that."

Guy finished his stew and pushed the bowl away. He wiped his mouth with the back of his hand and emptied the tankard. "Another!" he called, setting the mug aside as the old woman rushed over to collect the bowl and to refill his ale.

"Perhaps you should return to London so another—more honorable—knight can assume this quest as you seem loath to act in a manner befitting your station."

Slowly, he turned, taking in her enraged beauty. The fullness of her lips thinned as she pressed them together. Her hazel eyes flickered with distaste as he leaned close. But to her credit, she did not pull away.

He knew little of her situation, other than her plea to the king and the brief explanation she gave the garrison. But there was something in the way she spoke that told him there was more—possibly quite a bit more—to the story than she offered.

This mission was exactly what he required. Her mystery would unravel at his fingertips and no other's.

"You know nothing of me, vixen. *Nothing.*"

"I have no desire to."

Such defiance. It radiated from her, as bright and

effervescent as her physical beauty. A rare jewel hidden from view of the world. A wildflower planted in a bed of roses. She knew not her effect on him, and he would never tell.

"Pity," he teased. "If we were to share a bed, you could learn all sorts of…intimate things about me."

"Take the damned room," she growled. "I shall share a bed with my maid."

Guy ignored a pang of disappointment. "Suit yourself."

Mistress Marian finished her meal and stood as the old woman returned with more ale. "Might I see the room now?"

"Aye." The woman set down the tankard and led her away.

His heart twisted at her absence. He enjoyed their banter. It was quite evident she did not like or trust him. Perhaps it was for the best. There would be complications if he pursued her.

The more time he spent in her company, the more he longed to pluck this delicate flower for his own. If he were a chivalrous knight, he would pledge himself to her protection.

But he was not. And she would decline purely out of spite.

One truth he could not ignore—he would protect her, and it would come at a cost to her. Would she be willing to pay? Or would he take payment by force?

Chapter Three

After their encounter at the inn, Marian kept her distance from Sir Guy.

His actions spoke of a dark and troubled mind, a man shrouded in secrecy and shadows. Warily, she watched him from a distance over the past fortnight in an attempt to better understand the knight sent to protect her family and friends.

They would arrive at her father's castle by nightfall. Even now, they were traversing her father's holdings. Summer had arrived in full splendor with thick trees lining the road and wildflowers littering the meadows. Listening to birds sing in the distance, she admired the familiar landscape and basked in memories of home.

But even in the light of their imminent arrival, she could not shake the oppressive presence of the boorish knight, hanging like a thundercloud over their party.

Sir Guy Silverthorne had been correct. He was not a good man. Nor was he a kind one. His actions demonstrated it day after day. It began long before the night at the inn when he stole her room. From their first meeting at court, he had proved to be a most disagreeable man. Handsome to a fault but selfish and vain as well as arrogant.

His callous disregard for her well-being and that of her traveling companions had soured her on his company. When he threatened to kill a thief without hesitation, she recognized darkness in his soul.

What had he seen in his life to cause such a tear in his conscience? What possible torment must a man endure to blacken his soul to the point he could bloody his hands without regret? The man refused to speak to her beyond teasing remarks bordering on impropriety. The rest of his time was spent on horseback, brooding and surly.

There would be no answer from him. He kept his own council and maintained a calculated distance from the group. Even the men in the garrison whispered about their leader. Some of them had served with him before, but their stories faded to dull whispers when she approached. So she hid in the shadows, hoping to hear something that would better help her uncover the mystery surrounding the dark knight.

Alas, her subterfuge had garnered no fruitful information.

What she did gain, however, were small glimpses of his exploits. Places he had been, conflicts in which he'd fought. He had previously spent time at the border, fighting reivers in the east. This explained the king's quick and decisive selection. Judging from the pieces of conversation, his impact in the region had decimated the reivers, and whispers of his unorthodox methods terrified any who might try to fill the positions left vacant.

The *Grim Knight* they called him. An apt name to be sure, but mysteriously vague. There must be more to the stories than what she had learned from whispers of conversations stolen in passing. How to unearth them without confronting him directly seemed to be the pressing issue.

"Mistress Marian." A deep voice interrupted her thoughts.

His black stallion came alongside her, bearing its rider as though summoned from her thoughts. She looked at him, her lips pursed, assessing with a critical eye.

He held fast under her scrutiny, his expression unreadable. Those haunted eyes narrowed before turning to the road ahead.

"When we arrive, I shall require private quarters."

Marian scoffed. "Is it not enough for you to demand my room at the inn and steal away from our company after we make camp? Now you require special consideration for your accommodation at *my* home?"

"Aye." He offered nothing more, keeping his attention fixed on the path before them. "And if you wish for my aid, you will personally see to my requests."

She bristled at his arrogance. "I am not some poor servant to command at your whim."

"I serve at the command of the king. If you wish for my compliance, I have certain requirements that must be met."

Fury raged through her. "You place these stipulations upon me *now*? When we are nearly at my father's door?" Her grip tightened on the reins. It took all her restraint not to kick her horse into a gallop, to leave him behind to find his own way.

Sir Guy said nothing and rode silently beside her. He seemed wholly unbothered at his impertinent request.

"You require my presence and my skills, Mistress Marian."

His voice grated on what propriety remained in her.

"It would serve you well to remember, 'tis *you* who needs me."

Unable to bear his presence a moment longer, she kicked her horse's flanks and set off at a canter. The wind caught the edges of her veil, and she tugged it free, which allowed her to breathe. The long coil of her braid lay against her back, soft tendrils pulling free to tickle her face. She pushed them back and urged her mount faster.

As she went further along the path, the stone walls of her father's keep came into view in the distance. Relief filled her at the sight of it standing tall and strong in the sunlight. The closer she came, the more her resolve settled.

If he would demand boons for his service, she would see to the protection of her father's holding herself. She had no use for the Grim Knight or for his band of soldiers. Her trip to London to petition the king had been a monumental waste of resources and precious time. All of the responsibility would fall to her yet again. Until this moment, she had held out hope someone would come to her aid.

But that dream died the moment Sir Guy Silverthorne stepped into her life.

As she approached the gate, she called to the guards to move them to action. Certain of her identity, a guard shouted to open the gate. Her horse danced, bursting with energy at being home. She patted his neck and urged him forward when the portcullis opened.

She wove through the outer bailey and ventured into the

keep. When she reached the inner bailey, she dismounted and stroked the gelding's muzzle.

"Extra rations for you, Red." Marian handed the reins to a page. "See to it he is properly tended."

"Of course, my lady." The page bowed and led the horse into the stable.

Without waiting for the rest of the company, she strode to the door to the great hall. She needed to speak with her father before the Grim Knight and his garrison arrived.

Greeting the servants, she strode through the great hall and climbed the stairs to her father's chamber at the back of the keep. When she reached the door, she paused, taking a deep breath and tucking a stray hair behind her ear.

She knocked, then waited for his summons.

"Enter."

Upon opening the door, she faltered when she found her father sitting at the window overlooking the forest. Had his health improved?

He turned when she stepped into the room. "Daughter." He crossed the room, reaching for her. "I hoped you would return soon."

"Father." She embraced him, overjoyed to see him up and moving instead of confined to his bed.

"How fared you on your journey?" He drew back to study her face.

"The king heard my petition and granted my request for aid. He sent a small garrison, led by a knight." She purposely left out the details, hoping she could salvage what scraps she had been offered.

"A wonderous report." He beamed with pride. The gray at his temples made his face pale, but splotches of color high in his cheeks showed his good humor. Mayhap he was truly recovering from the mysterious illness that had plagued him for so long.

"Where are our esteemed guests?"

His question broke through her thoughts. "They will be arriving any moment, Father. I rode ahead to give you the news and prepare the way for them."

"Go down and greet them." He shooed her to the door. "I shall be down directly."

"Do you think that wise, Father? Your health…" She worried her lip between her teeth.

"I will greet our guests and extend them every courtesy." He reached for the pull to summon the servants. "Now go. I shall join you momentarily."

"Aye, Father." Marian kissed his cheek before departing.

In the great hall, she found Mae, the housekeeper, and gave instruction for the incoming guests, begrudgingly securing a private room for the Grim Knight. Unfortunately, the only available room was next to her own. The thought of having him so close left a bitter taste in her mouth.

But better to keep her enemies closer than her allies.

After securing the required provisions for the garrison, she found space for them in the soldiers' quarters that had been abandoned the previous year when reivers waged their vicious assault and killed most of the soldiers. The rest deserted their posts, save for a small group of honorable men who stayed and found lodgings elsewhere.

Just as she re-entered the outer bailey, her traveling party came through the gate. The chatter of those who worked in the keep swirled around her, curiosity blossoming into hope at the sight of the garrison. Perhaps her trip to London had not been in vain.

Sir Guy appeared in the crowd at the rear of the procession. He slipped from his horse and handed the reins to the same page who had taken her mount earlier. After a quick exchange, the page led the horse toward the stables.

Marian watched as he strode through the crowd. She sucked in a breath when he spotted her. Taking a moment to steady herself, she stepped into his path.

"My father awaits you in the great hall."

"Very well." He inclined his head and gestured for her to lead the way.

Aware of his presence behind her, she hastened her pace. The quicker she dispensed with formalities, the faster she could deal with more pressing issues. Her men would be curious about the return of their fearless leader, and she needed to warn them of the Grim Knight's presence.

Her father waited in the great hall, sitting in his favorite chair at the far end of the room. He stood as she approached with Sir Guy trailing behind.

"Sir Guy, I would like to make you known to my father, Jonas Ravenwood, the Baron Ravinell. Father, this is Sir Guy Silverthorne, the king's representative." Marian stepped to the side.

Sir Guy bowed to the baron. "My lord."

"Rise, good sir." The baron stepped down from the dais and studied the knight as he rose to his full height. "Silverthorne…" He tapped his jaw thoughtfully. "Do they not call you the Grim Knight?"

A muscle in Sir Guy's jaw clenched. "They do."

"Your reputation precedes you." The old man clapped his hands one time. "I have heard of your exploits. Impressive. The very mention of your name will send the bastards running."

"As they should." Sir Guy bowed his head. "I must see to my men, if you will excuse me." He pivoted to face Marian. "Would you be so kind as to accompany me, my lady?"

"Go with him, Marian. Give him all he requires."

Her mouth dropped open, but she snapped it closed when she noticed amusement dancing in Sir Guy's eyes.

"Very well," she ground out. "Come along."

The sun dipped behind the trees, and it would be dark soon. She led him through the bailey without a word, eager to be out of his presence. When she reached the soldiers' quarters, she stopped at the door and turned to him. "The garrison will stay here. If you will excuse me, I must tend to other matters before dark."

"Where are my quarters?" he asked, stepping close, crowding her.

"The housekeeper is preparing your room." Her eyes narrowed. "Pardon me."

She tried to duck around him, but he blocked her retreat

with one arm.

"Such haste to be away from me."

"There are many things requiring my attention, sir, and you are not one of them." She pushed against him.

He dropped his arm and stepped aside to allow her to pass.

"You cannot avoid me forever, my lady."

His haunting words followed her to the postern gate.

By the time she reached a small shelter tucked into a ridge, darkness had settled across the sky. She knocked twice and murmured, "Butcher."

At the code word, the door swung open. She stepped through the hidden door and stood beside a small, shaggy-haired man.

"You have returned. Saints be praised."

"'Tis good to see you, Samuel." Her heart warmed.

He led her into the room, beyond a dark curtain, to where a fire burned in a tiny pit and the scent of roasted meat filled the air.

"Mistress Marian." Another man stood, pulling his cap from his head.

"Jack." Her gaze drifted over the small group around the fire. Their somber expressions filled her with dread. "What has happened?"

"The reivers." Jack spoke for the group. "They came while you were in London. Raided the village just our side of the border. Stole all the animals, burned the buildings."

"Killed everyone," Samuel added.

The room stilled.

Grief choked her. Tears stung her eyes. *Curse them. Curse all of them.* "I never should have left."

"You could not have stopped them." Jack met her gaze. "None of us could."

"This needs to end." Her voice quivered with rage and frustration. "The king granted aid, a small garrison led by a knight."

Hope filled their expressions.

"The Grim Knight." The moment she said the words, the

mood in the room shifted from hope back to despair.

"He kills for sport," Jack said, his voice low. "Not just reivers. *All* outlaws. By special command of the king."

Marian suppressed a shiver. "Is this not to our benefit?"

"He will kill them, my lady. And he will kill *us*." Jack sighed.

"You have done nothing but protect what belongs to my father."

"Aye, but we are outlaws in our own right." Jack hung his head.

"We cannot surrender. Not now. Not after what they have done." Fire burned inside her, ignited by a spark of vengeance, driven by a deeper purpose. "Our people deserve protection."

The men nodded.

"Tomorrow eve, meet me here to devise a plan." She took measure of each man, finding determination in their eyes.

After a few moments, she took her leave, slipping into the night. The moon slowly climbed in the sky and aided her progress along the narrow path as she returned to the keep.

The postern guard permitted her entry, and she quietly slipped through the kitchen, not disturbing the servants as they worked. She wove through them, smiling, snatching bites along the way.

She passed her maid and requested a bath be drawn in her chamber. Eager to be away from crowds and prying eyes, she made her way up the stairs to her chamber. When she reached the threshold to her safe haven, a voice drifted from the shadows.

"Where have you been hiding?"

Marian spun, pressing a hand to her racing heart. "Sir Guy." She pressed her back to her door as he stepped into the flickering candlelight. "You gave me a fright."

"Is this your chamber?" He rested his hand on the wood beside her head, crowding her, eliminating the space between them with the heat of his body and his sheer breadth. The clean scent of soap filled her head with images quite unbecoming of a lady—the Grim Knight, completely bare, lounging in a tub of hot water beside the fire.

"Aye." She swallowed hard, banishing the unwelcome thoughts.

"How intriguing." He looked down the hall to her left. "You placed me in a room near yours."

"To ensure you mind your manners while under my father's roof. I will not tolerate torment of my servants to serve your lustful needs."

"Perhaps you wish to keep…my lustful needs for yourself, my lady." His eyes shone with mischief in the dancing light.

"There is nothing about your company I enjoy, sir."

"A shame." His lips curled in a satisfied grin. "Your father proclaimed you would show me the area that I might better understand what I am sworn to protect."

Her breath caught when his gaze dropped briefly to her lips.

"He seemed quite adamant you are the only one qualified to properly *educate* me."

The implication of his words created a flurry of uncertainty in her mind. Was he toying with her? Teasing her? Surely, this was a trap, a way to bait her into retaliation. She loathed him with a passion far outweighing any possible temptation.

Marian drew a small dagger from her pocket and pressed it to his neck. "I will not be trifled with, sir. I am no whore to succumb to your charm."

"Ah, but you admit I have charm?"

Her scowl deepened as she pressed the blade against his skin. He hissed, and his smile widened.

"You have the charm of a serpent."

Sir Guy stepped back, removing his hand from the door, his heat retreating with him. She dropped the dagger to her side, stunned at the shift in the air around her.

"My lady." He bowed stiffly and strode down the hall, leaving her to tremble in his wake.

What is this sorcery? Why must he torment me in such a manner?

Shaking, Marian opened the door and entered her warm chamber. With a sigh, she sank into a chair beside the hearth, her gaze lost in the flames.

"What am I to do?" she muttered aloud, searching her mind

for a solution to the problems before her. How could she avoid Sir Guy and his soldiers while still leading her men? Perhaps asking help from the king had been rash.

Yet she knew, deep in her heart, she could not do this alone. She needed *someone*.

But not Sir Guy Silverthorne, not the Grim Knight.

Anyone but him.

Chapter Four

Knowing only a single wall separated them drove Guy to the edge of madness. He spent half the night seated beside the fire with a goblet of wine, staring at the barrier between them. Not only the thick stone, but the seemingly unsurmountable chasm of status and experiences. How in the devil had she managed to ensnare his curiosity? His reluctant admiration?

It itched beneath his skin, this unfamiliar sensation. In the past, women had been a means to an end. A pleasurable distraction for a short period of time. Nothing more. No one had enticed him with such a burning need to unravel mysteries and secret desires. No one until Marian. He longed to pluck each thought from her mind, to see beyond her vehement loathing of him.

She abhorred him, that much was clear. He could not blame her; his past actions placed him beyond salvation. Yet she did not know the extent of his depravity, the depths to which he had lowered himself to guarantee his position in the king's favor. There was not a soul alive who knew the truth.

And he planned to keep it that way.

Rumors about him quelled the insatiable curiosity of the masses and barely nicked the armor protecting his past and his heart.

Mistress Marian had secrets of her own. Judging from the fierceness of her personality, there were many things she kept locked away from public view. It ensured her survival. Which only enhanced his interest. She intrigued him to the point of distraction.

He understood the desire to hide, to keep part of himself tucked away from view, safely protected from destruction. They were a kindred pair, even if she did not know it.

Exhaustion pulled him to the bed, but he found no rest. By

dawn, his restlessness had festered into irritation.

Guy relinquished his bed and dressed in a simple black tunic and hose, complemented by blackened leather boots. Such dark clothes would absorb the heat of the sun, but he rarely wore any article of clothing that was not black. The color matched his mood and deterred conversation when paired with his perpetual scowl…an observation he'd discovered and eagerly embraced at a young age.

When he reached the bailey, the soldiers were milling about. The captain spied him and sheathed his sword as Guy approached.

"Captain," Guy said, his voice firm but quiet. "Split the men into groups of three or four and have them scout the area. Take note of any disturbance. I expect a full report by nightfall."

"As you command, Sir Guy."

"Do not reveal your station or where you are staying. You are merely travelers passing through." Guy's gaze drifted over the men saddling horses and sharpening blades. "They will learn the truth soon enough, but until then, do not offer more information than necessary. Your mission is to unearth anything that could lead us to the reivers."

The captain bowed and retreated to instruct the men.

Guy strode across the bailey to ensure his stallion had received adequate provisions. The beast could be stubborn and unruly, much like his rider. But when he ducked into the stalled area, he could not find the familiar black head among the horses. A groom came out of one of the stalls.

"Boy, where have you stored my mount?"

The lad spun around, startled by Guy's appearance, his eyes wide. "At the far end, sir. He bit the stablemaster, so we moved him away from the other horses."

Guy shook his head and followed the lad to a corner stall, which proved larger than the other stalls and gave his stallion more room. 'Twas almost as if the beast knew his attack on the stablemaster would earn him a quiet place. When Guy leaned against the stall door, the stallion turned and softly whickered. The stable lad backed away, retreating to his duties.

"Getting into trouble already, Nix?" Guy asked softly, rubbing the horse's soft muzzle.

The black beast defiantly tossed his head and pawed at the ground.

"Later, I will take you out," he whispered. "Enjoy your rest while you can."

The groom reappeared with fresh hay and grain. Nix greeted him with a nicker and stole a mouthful of hay from the boy's arms.

"Feed him well and he will not bite."

"Aye, sir."

With a farewell pat, he turned away from the horse. Pressing issues attended to, he could now focus on his next challenge. Mistress Marian.

Her father had assured him his daughter would take him on a tour of the keep and surrounding area, as well as the local village. Perhaps that was what had kept him awake most of the night, the promise of spending uninterrupted time with this woman who so thoroughly vexed him. Or it could have been their encounter outside her chamber.

Saints, he could still smell sweet rosewater mixed with smoke he'd detected when he leaned close. Her dark locks had lain in a loose plait over her shoulder with soft tendrils framing her face, highlighting her eyes and the soft bow of her plush lips.

Restraint be damned, he wanted to taste her.

His cock ached even now at the memory of her. It hardened further when he thought of her fire and the press of her dagger against his throat. Such passion. It flickered in her eyes when she stared him down, her threat lingering between them.

With a grunt, he shoved away the memory. It would do him no good to dwell upon it. Later, in the comfort of his chambers, he could indulge the fantasy to his heart's content. The mission before him was not to conquer the Mistress Marian, but to ensure her safety by slaying the reivers terrorizing the baron's holding. Perhaps his success would garner him a kind word or a gentle touch from the lady.

His stomach growled, demanding sustenance. He found

some morsels in the great hall to satisfy his need. When he finished the final bites, he glimpsed a flash of green from the corner of his eye.

He slowly turned, and the rush of desire he felt the night before crashed over him. Mistress Marian crossed the great hall, the gold edges of her green gown flashing beneath the sunlight streaming through the windows. As the day before, her hair lay uncovered but pinned in an intricate braid coiled around her head. His fingers itched, aching to pull the pins free, to let the mass tumble around her shoulders. He longed to wrap the braid around his hand, to hold her fast as he stole her breath with wandering kisses along her throat.

As if he had spoken his desires aloud, she looked in his direction.

"Does something plague you, sir?" Mistress Marian asked.

"Nay." He rose to his feet.

"Very well. Follow me. There is much to see, and daylight runs scarce."

Guy smothered a smile before it could steal across his lips. She could not possibly know he had woken before dawn and had already tended to his men as well as his horse. Instead of baiting her, he fell into step behind her, quietly admiring the gentle curve of her neck and the sway of her backside beneath her skirts.

The sun had barely crested the tips of the trees when they mounted their horses. Nix danced beneath him, irritated at the gelding being allowed to lead. Once they were free of the keep, he brought his stallion beside her.

"We shall take the path through the village and return through the forest." Her lilting voice had a dagger's edge. 'Twas obvious she held him in no regard, especially after their encounter last eve.

He listened as she spoke, soaking up the words and their meanings. Deep inside his mind, he allowed himself a small concession to imagine her lips engaged in a more pleasurable activity.

She continued, unaware of his musings. "My father's lands run along the border with Scotland to the north. Lord de

Bough's holdings lie to the east, and Lord Hayworth's are to the west and south."

"Have you spoken with them about the reivers?" Guy asked, pulling his thoughts from the dangerous mire.

"I have. They assured me of support in stopping the attacks."

"And yet, you had to petition the king for soldiers to deal with the ongoing threat to your father's lands? If you have their support, they should supply men and resources to bring an end to these attacks." He studied her and noted a deepening frown.

"They claim they have not had as many problems with the reivers as we have." Her tone dropped lower. "It is odd."

"Indeed." He tucked the information in the back of his mind and pressed on with his inquiry. "Have *you* encountered the reivers?"

"Nay," she replied quickly.

Almost too quickly.

"'Tis a good thing. They can be heartless and violent."

"I have heard similar." She eyed him for a moment before returning her attention to the path. "I have also heard you have dealt with their kind on previous occasion?"

"Aye." Flashes of violent memories assailed him, but he pushed them aside and tightened his hold on the reins.

"Yet you survived?"

He nodded, unwilling to feed her curiosity if she would not ask him directly.

"You are skilled with a blade?" she asked.

"And a bow." He met her gaze. "Have you trained with either?"

"Of course not." She straightened in the saddle. "A lady would never engage in such things."

Her hollow protest echoed between them. While he could not judge her sincerity in other matters, he saw a lie in her vehement response. She could fight—he would stake his knighthood on it—but with bow or blade, he could not decipher. Perhaps he could put it to the test when they returned to the keep.

"I will teach you."

"If I wished to learn, I could certainly find someone worthy to instruct me." She sniffed with disdain.

"No one could give you a more *thorough* instruction than I, my lady."

Her gasp disappeared on the wind, but knowing his well-placed shot struck the intended mark left him preening. Teasing her in such a manner invigorated him in a way he would never have imagined. The volley of barbs kept him sharp. He craved more. If only he could convince her to his way of thinking, entice her to embrace her dark nature. The carnal desire and bloodthirst that dwelled deep in the shadowed recesses of every mind.

"The village." She cleared her throat and pointed.

A small group of buildings appeared on the horizon. With each step, they grew in size and breadth. His gaze skimmed over the buildings and the people as the horses carried them into the village. There was nothing special or gaudy about the hamlet. He had seen hundreds of villages of similar size and build across the country and beyond. Each carried its own special touch, but nothing by which he remembered them.

They all meant nothing.

As they wandered through the village and around the forest, he listened to her tell stories of the people and places within her domain. While he took careful note of everything she said, the only thing that truly struck him was *her*.

Mistress Marian was a lady of the people. Dedicated to their well-being and safety. She thrived in the role of patroness and guardian of peace. He heard every concern in currents beneath her actual words. It touched his cold heart to hear how much she cared.

He wished he could say the same, but there was no compassion left in him. Whatever humanity had resided within his soul had withered and died when he was a child. When he watched his family burn at the hand of pillaging thieves.

By the time they reached the keep, the sun hung heavy in the western sky, turning the blues into hues of pink and orange. He dismounted after her, noting that his men had returned from their earlier mission.

"Come, I will give you a tour."

"I will find my own way around the keep." He bowed.

"Very well." She bristled at his clipped response, and without waiting for an explanation, she retreated into the great hall.

A strange urge to follow her, to apologize tugged at his conscience. He clenched his hands into fists.

Focus.

He spotted the captain speaking with a comely maiden and redirected his irritation. "Captain," he said, approaching the man. The maiden took one look at him and bolted toward the kitchen entrance.

"Sir." The man straightened instantly.

"Report."

"Aye, sir." He led Guy to a shadowed nook in the stone wall. "The men all report sightings of the reivers over the past fortnight." He kept his voice low. "They also heard stories of a separate group of outlaws living in the forest."

"Reivers *and* a band of outlaws?" Guy's scowl deepened. "What have these outlaws done?"

"They are thieves."

Guy grasped the man by the tunic and shook him. "*Who* are they stealing from?"

"No one knows for certain, sir."

"What do you mean?"

"These outlaws roam the forest, but no one has actually seen them take anything, save for wandering livestock." The captain licked his lips, his voice growing stronger. "But there is something even stranger."

Guy inclined his head but said nothing.

"There are rumors from the holdings of the neighboring lords."

Guy's eyes narrowed.

"Their lands are not similarly affected. The reivers *only* target Ravenwood's lands."

"Indeed." Guy released the man. "We shall have to

investigate thoroughly."

"Aye, sir." The captain straightened his tunic. "I shall send men out on the morrow to gather more information."

With a nod, Guy dismissed the captain and leaned against the stone.

A lovely, fiery maiden, a band of outlaws, and violent reivers. Perhaps there was something on this border worth his time after all.

Chapter Five

After nearly a sennight with Sir Guy at the keep, Marian found herself longing for the blissful obscurity of the forest and the unwavering support of her men. He stalked her like a shadow, appearing at random moments, keeping his distance, yet watching with a sharp eye.

Curse him for his persistence. Had he no other task to keep him occupied? Must he constantly trail her, like a wolf stalking its prey? It was quite wearisome.

Upon rising early, Marian made her way to the kitchen, hoping to slip through the postern gate unnoticed. She had neglected her men long enough. They needed a plan to gain advantage over the reivers.

Her thought process had been simple. If she and her band of men exerted their influence on the region, stealing paltry coin from traveling nobles, antagonizing local gentry, attacking only those who were hostile to her people, perhaps the reivers would see them as competitors and target her and her men instead of innocent people.

She knew her plan would work, if only she could free herself from the confines of the keep long enough to stir up trouble. But when her father sent petitions to the king via messenger and they returned unanswered, he charged her with the mission to personally deliver his request.

They both understood the delicacy and danger of such a quest, but she could not disobey her father's direction. When his health deteriorated to the point he was unable to travel beyond the confines of his keep, the responsibility fell to her to represent him and the barony.

This threw her plan into chaos. Her men had kept watch during her journey to London, and their quiet observation allowed the reivers to again encroach on her father's lands. She needed to direct the reivers' attention away from the people. The only way to do this was to assume the hood and take to the forest.

Which was impossible with the hovering presence of the Grim Knight.

When she reached the postern gate, elation filled her. She would be free as soon as she reached the trees.

"My lady, where do you venture in such haste?" Sir Guy's voice stopped her.

Curse him a thousand times over.

"I have an urgent message to deliver," she lied, turning to face him.

"Send a messenger." He stepped from the shadows. The morning sun cast his features into stark contrasts. He looked more like a predator than usual, with flashing teeth and narrowed eyes.

"'Tis a personal matter. I must deliver this missive myself." Her hand clenched the iron bar.

"Then I shall accompany you." He rested his hand upon the hilt of the blade against his hip.

She bristled but managed to retain her calm. "Such gallantry is unnecessary, sir. I am perfectly capable of delivering a message on my own."

With two steps, he closed the gap between them. She pressed her back to the gate and inhaled deeply, bracing for a fight.

"With such threat beyond these walls, 'twould be unwise to allow you to venture out on your own. Should you encounter reivers, they will show you no mercy." He held his ground. "If they uncover your identity, you are as good as dead."

Marian scoffed. "How can you be so certain of my fate?"

His eyes darkened, as if overtaken by a storm. "I have seen firsthand the vicious carnage of reivers. They do not make concessions. They pillage, plunder, rape, and murder. They will not hesitate to take anything they want."

She shivered at the way his gaze drifted down her form before returning to her eyes. His words did not frighten her. She knew these things already and did not fear the reivers. She was fully prepared to face them and embrace the consequences of such an encounter.

But the heat and hatred in Sir Guy's burning gaze left her trembling. What horrors he must have endured to be so callous and cold.

"I do not fear them." Marian licked her lips and lifted her chin.

"You should."

"I am perfectly capable of protecting myself."

His laugh stunned her. The deep throaty sound echoed around them.

"You said yourself, you have no training with sword or bow." He cocked his head, studying her carefully. "How could you possibly protect yourself with your tiny dagger?"

She warmed under his scrutiny. He baited her, teased her. Tormented her with his persistent presence and relentless pride. Sir Guy was neither a good man nor a chivalrous knight. His protection and his concern were not born of good intentions. He demanded *something* for his service. Her mind refused to allow her to pursue the thought further.

When she did not reply, he reached for her. Quick as a flash of lightening, she drew her dagger and again pressed it to his throat.

"I assure you, sir. I am quite capable of protecting myself."

His eyes closed and a wolfish smile curved his lips.

A soft chuckle spilled from his throat even as her dagger dug into his flesh. One small twist, and she could end his life. His scent surrounded her—leather, horses, smoke with a hint of something dark beneath the surface. She readjusted her grip on the weapon, shaking the distraction from her mind.

Sir Guy seized the opening, grabbing her wrist and spinning her around. Her arm twisted, and the dagger fell to the ground. He pinned her arm against his chest and pulled up. She winced at the pain radiating through her arm.

Her moment of weakness had paved the way for him to retaliate. Curse him. She knew better than to allow even the smallest opening. A whimper escaped her when he wrapped his other arm around her waist and tightened his hold. She pushed against him, writhing and bucking against his hold. The movement only intensified the agonizing pain in her arm and shoulder. Fighting him was like charging a hundred-year-old oak in the forest; he stood unmovable and proud. Panting, she stilled.

His warmth seeped into her, and she closed her eyes in an effort to ward off the effect it had on her wits.

"Well now, vixen, for all your fire, you are still vulnerable." His breath caressed her cheek.

Her eyes flew open and she pushed at the arm locked around her waist. "Release me."

"Concede."

"I concede," she hissed, wanting nothing more than to put distance between them. His proximity addled her.

Slowly, he released the arm twisted behind her back, but he did not remove the hold on her waist.

"I said…" Her voice trembled. Digging deep, she drew strength from within and steadied her tone. "Release me."

A soft exhalation of breath tickled her cheek as the pressure relented. She wrenched herself away and gripped her aching arm, rubbing the joint to encourage blood flow. Marian glared at this man who seemed nonplussed by what had just transpired.

He plucked her dagger from the dirt and wiped it on his thigh to clean the blade.

"The next time you draw this blade on me, you better use it." He held it out by the blade, hilt facing her.

"I shall. Of that, you can be certain." She snatched the dagger, hoping the edge would bite his flesh as she did so.

"There you are!" The steward stepped out of the kitchen doorway. "Your father wishes to speak with you, my lady."

"Very well." She tucked her dagger away and strode past Sir Guy. The insufferable knight stood unmoving, watching her, his eyes dark and unreadable.

As she entered the kitchens, the weight of their interaction lay heavy on her shoulders. What game was he playing? Why had he taken a personal interest in her safety?

The questions lingered in her mind through the day. Even as she spoke with her father, her thoughts drifted to the Grim Knight. She would need to find a new way to escape the keep without him following.

Perhaps he needed something to engage his attention. Even a simple distraction could give her an opportunity to escape. A plan formed in her mind.

Later that day, she received a cryptic message from her men, delivered by a visiting merchant. They wanted to meet that night after full dark.

With whispered instructions, she charged her maid with simple instructions. Sir Guy required a diversion, and she knew just how to provide it.

Chapter Six

Whispered lies often lead merry chases. As the sun dropped below the trees, Guy relaxed in his saddle as his horse ambled down a narrow path through the forest near the border. 'Twas the first day he had spent outside the keep, free of the confines of stone walls and the overwhelming presence of Mistress Marian.

After spending much of his time focused on the baron's daughter, Guy had made a shocking discovery. He *relished* the stolen moments, exchanging witty banter and barbed insults with the vivacious Mistress Marian. This realization should have been a sign to direct his attention to more pressing matters, such as the reivers hiding in shadows. Or the rumors of this mysterious band of outlaws. Neither group had made their presence known to him. His men had patrolled the baron's holdings for nigh on ten nights with nothing but whispers and rumors to guide them.

The evidence of past raids littered the baron's lands. Homes burned to the ground. Fields decimated. Livestock stolen…and whatever could not be carried lay slaughtered, scattered through green pastures.

Some of the soldiers overheard the maids talking in hushed, fearful tones. They spoke of concern for families in the villages. Guy took it upon himself to survey the damage and personally assess the threat. While his men were competent, he trusted no one, not even the captain who attested to the carnage ravaging the area. Yet he loathed the idea of leaving Mistress Marian unsupervised.

Guy ventured further along the path, taking in the landscape and villages, both to the east and west of the baron's borders. What he saw left him with more questions than answers. The reivers and outlaws targeted only those under the protection of Baron Ravinell. The baron had an enemy, that much was certain.

The destruction thrust upon the area was the work of reivers. He had seen similar devastation before when dealing with reivers to the east.

But they did not discriminate against specific holdings. They looted and pillaged along the border without regard for who owned the land.

That, in itself, left him with a burning desire to uncover the mystery at the heart of these attacks. It had been too long since he had faced a foe worth fighting, and the reivers were a threat he longed to encounter face-to-face.

The unusual band of outlaws, however, were an inconvenience more than a threat. Not that he had any solid evidence to back this assumption, but years of service to the king in battle had prepared him to embrace whatever challenge crossed his path. Being able to recognize a foe as well as their true intentions was a skill earned only through careful cultivation.

Ahead, the path split, one trail leading to the keep, the other north to the Scottish border. He followed the one going south to a small meadow. Darkness surrounded him, the soft glow of the moon filtering through the trees. Nix whickered softly.

"Easy boy." He patted the stallion's neck and urged him onward.

A soft rustling in the trees to his right brought him up short. He reined the horse to a halt and listened. The sound came again, closer this time.

A frustrated hiss echoed in the dense foliage.

Nix danced beneath him, clearly agitated, ready to bolt.

"Who goes there?" Guy growled, resting his hand on the hilt of his blade.

A horse lunged from the thicket ahead. The dark form galloped along the path in the pale moonlight. From this angle, he could not be sure whether it bore a rider. His thighs tensed as he braced to set Nix in pursuit.

An arrow whistled past his head, striking the tree behind him. His head whipped around as he searched the trees, but he saw nothing to betray an archer. Another arrow slipped past his shoulder and drove into the ground.

Nix loosed a whinny and reared, throwing Guy from the saddle.

He collided with the hard dirt and winced at the pain vibrating through his hip and back. Nix darted forward, galloping after the other horse.

Guy scrambled to his feet, ignoring the ache in his body. He drew his sword and crept closer to the brush to shield himself from another arrow.

His heart pounded in his ears, mixing with the songs of night birds and insects. A gentle breeze drifted over him, ruffling his hair. He pushed through the foliage, taking each step with measured care.

The attacker certainly had the advantage, but it would prove more difficult to shoot him if he was covered by thick brush and low branches. His boots crunched in the soft undergrowth.

He listened carefully, searching for any indication of the shooter's location. Perhaps the man had already fled. Guy pushed deeper into the trees, his blade drawn and ready.

A heavy body collided with his back, knocking him forward. He stumbled a few steps before righting himself against the trunk of a tree. Spinning to face his assailant, he brandished his sword and bared his teeth.

The thick shadows shifted, and a form stepped into a thin shaft of moonlight. Clad in black with a deep hood hiding his features, the attacker held his own sword at the ready.

"What have we here?" Guy shoved away from the tree, prepared to fight. "Only an outlaw would hide beneath a hood."

The man dipped a halfhearted bow but said nothing.

"'Tis unwise to cross blades with me." Guy closed the gap between them and tapped his blade to the outlaw's. "I shall give you only one chance to surrender before I run you through."

The outlaw swung his sword, bringing it against Guy's in a clash of steel.

"Very well," Guy said with a grunt.

He launched into motion.

They danced, parrying and ducking beneath the sweep of blades. Diving in and out of shafts of moonlight and shadow, he chased the outlaw's attacks with counters of his own. The sounds of panting breaths and shuffling feet mingled with the distinctive *clang* of each strike.

Guy slipped behind a tree, barely evading the tip of his opponent's sword as it arced toward him. A soft curse echoed in the air.

Guy chuckled at his opponent's vehement reaction. It bolstered his confidence, and he rushed forward, pushing the outlaw back until the man was pinned against another tree, Guy's blade against his neck. The sharp edge dug deeper as he leaned into it.

The outlaw sucked in a breath and flinched under Guy's hold. 'Twas the first time he had placed his hands upon the man. He had expected more muscle, more strength beneath the black garments.

The delicate build betrayed not a man…nay, it could not be so.

"A woman?" His surprised response broke the silence, and he eased back slightly.

The outlaw broke his grip and shoved Guy enough to slide free. She spun, dragging her blade across his arm. It sliced easily through the thin fabric of his tunic, and warmth spread over his arm as the blood soaked the linen.

A frustrated growl ripped from his throat as he pivoted. The outlaw darted deeper into the forest, dodging around tall trees and behind the brush. He chased after her, determined to unmask this villainess who dared challenge him. His arm stung, but he pushed beyond the discomfort.

The forest grew thicker the deeper they ventured. No moonlight could break through the treetops. They stumbled along in darkness. Flashes of shadows danced before him, taunting him. A flicker of movement caught his eye.

In a burst of speed, he rushed ahead, breaking through the trees. He stumbled onto a narrow path, tripping over loose dirt. He spun, searching for the outlaw, but 'twas no use. She had fled.

"God's blood, teeth, and bones." He pushed his hair back and kicked at a tuft of grass.

A blinding burst of pain thundered through his skull. He pitched forward, collapsing in the dirt. His sword fell, useless, by his side. His vision danced with shadow and moonlight as a dark figure stepped into view. Guy studied dirty black boots, unable to focus on anything beyond them.

Then darkness claimed him.

When he woke, his head ached. Dried blood crusted his hair. He shifted to assess his wound but could not move his arms.

"What the devil?" He jerked and twisted, to no avail. The binds around his torso tightened with each twitch.

Guy leaned against the base of a tree and took in his surroundings. The sky overhead stretched in a predawn blue with orange glinting in the distance, illuminating the path in front of him. Should someone happen along, they would see him, bound to a tree, weak.

Nix would return to the keep. His men would search for him. They would find him thus.

He would be forced to endure the torment of their jests. He would tell them his own version of events, for there was no one to contradict him, lest the outlaw unmask herself.

He gritted his teeth and swore.

Curse the woman. She had seized the opportunity to escape and overpowered him with trickery. As time passed, he pondered the situation, taking measure of her actions against his own.

She had rendered him helpless with a blow to the back of the head. Having done so, she could have killed him. One well-placed thrust of her blade and she would have bested him forever.

Why had she not killed him?

The question nagged him as he watched the sun climb the horizon.

When the sound of hooves pounding the dirt reached his ears, he called out, hoping to catch the attention of whoever passed.

The captain and two men appeared around the corner and smothered their amused expressions at his withering glare. He offered no explanation as they cut through the ropes.

Released from his bonds, Guy took the captain's horse and rode posthaste to the keep. Only when he reached the privacy of his chambers did he allow himself to breathe deeply.

He attempted to pull his tunic off but winced at the pain in his arm. His fingers traced the strips of fabric binding his wound.

Not only was the outlaw a woman, but she bore a conscience.

What a foolish mistake on her part. When he uncovered her identity, he would do what she had refused to do. Mercy was a weakness he could ill afford.

She should have killed him when she had the chance.

Chapter Seven

Breathless and on foot, Marian reached the gate as sunlight was breaking the horizon. When the keep came into view, she sighed with relief. She ducked into a small hut at the edge of the forest, where she shed her dark garments and changed into a simple kirtle. Her neck burned when she pressed a dark swath of cloth to the place where his blade had nicked her skin.

Damn him. She tidied herself as best she could under the circumstances and tried to hide her injury. Perhaps a wimple would conceal it. She frowned. Wearing such contraptions left her twitching with discomfort. The warm summer air would stifle her if she attempted to conceal the wound.

She could not allow him to catch sight of the mark. Sir Guy was no fool. 'Twould not take more than a passing glimpse for him to ascertain the true identity of the outlaw he'd encountered during the night.

Marian collected her wits as she stepped into the early morning air. She could address the wound once she returned to the keep. Her maid, Anne, was an accomplished healer with knowledge of all manner of herbs and poultices. Together, they would concoct a way to hide the cut from prying eyes.

The guards exchanged a look of concern before one of them darted forward. "My lady. Are you well?"

"Aye." She laughed, though it sounded hoarse and broken.

"What happened?" He took her arm and escorted her through the gate, into the safety of the keep.

"A stag spooked my horse, and I fell."

He nodded, his lips set in a thin line. "When your horse returned without a rider, we were concerned for your welfare."

"I am perfectly well. There is no reason to fret." She lowered her voice. "Although, if you can, please keep this incident and my return from spreading. I do not wish to unduly alarm my father. His health has finally improved, and I do not wish it to deteriorate again because of my poor horsemanship."

The guard nodded. "As you wish, my lady."

"Gramercy." Marian offered her gratitude to the guard.

He opened the door to permit her entrance to the inner bailey. "Take care, my lady. The reivers will show no mercy should they capture you."

"I shall take better care in the future." She slipped through the door and made haste to her chambers.

Many of the servants were already milling about the keep. She smiled as she passed them, acting as though she had only been attending to duties within the sturdy stone walls. When she spied Anne outside her chambers, she nearly cried in relief.

Anne followed her into the room and closed the door. Marian turned, and her maid's eyes widened when she noticed the wound.

"The reivers?" she asked, gathering a small herbal kit tucked in Marian's wardrobe.

Marian shook her head. "Nay."

"Sit by the window," Anne instructed, her voice stern. "I have advised you a hundred times—do not venture into the woods after dark. Nothing good will come of it, should they capture you."

"It was not reivers."

"Who would dare attack a lady?" Anne gently peeled away the rag to reveal the wound.

"Sir Guy." Marian hissed at the sting as Anne cleaned the wound. Her confession hung between them.

"He set out to cause you harm?"

"'Tis complicated." Marian stared at the wall as Anne cleaned the wound before applying herbs. "I was hidden. My horse spooked and bolted, giving away my location."

She looked at Anne who worked quietly. The maid's lips were pressed together, as if she longed to chastise Marian for being so reckless.

"We fought. He caught me unaware." She gestured to her neck. "I paid him back in kind." A smile curved her lips at the memory. He had underestimated her. Most men did when they came against her in combat.

"My lady." Anne's words echoed like a mother's exasperated reprimand. "He could have killed you."

"Yet he did not." Marian straightened as Anne bandaged the wound. "Although *I* could have killed *him*. Easily."

"I take it he knows not the identity of his opponent." Anne tutted, unconvinced of the wisdom of these actions.

"Of course not. I took great care to ensure my face and voice remained concealed." Marian rose and pressed her hand to the bandage. She studied Anne's furrowed brow. "You disapprove of my behavior?"

"I worry for your safety, my lady. With so much turmoil in the region, my heart stops every time you leave the keep. Perhaps you should marry Graham de Bough…at least you would be protected."

"You mean locked away." Marian shook her head. "I shall not trade my freedom and my body for a false sense of security. A husband would not guarantee our protection."

Anne returned the herbs to the wooden box and closed the lid. "An alliance would strengthen your father's holdings."

"An alliance with whom? Lord Manning? He is more concerned with his horses than his people. And Lord de Bough, while chivalrous and wealthy, does not appeal to me in such a manner. He would never understand my needs or my desires."

"Such things are never guaranteed in a marriage." Anne placed the kit back in the wardrobe before selecting a clean gown for Marian.

"My father understood my mother's needs, her desires. He never stifled her under the yoke of society's expectations." Marian carefully removed her kirtle and laid it aside.

"Aye. They were a love match." Anne's wistful sigh filled the air. Silence fell between them as she helped Marian dress.

'Twas true; her parents wed for love. Their union had been unique. And yet, its rarity did not stop Marian from longing for a similar marriage. If she *had* to marry, it would be the only agreeable stipulation.

"Did you kill him?" Anne asked, putting the final touches to her ensemble.

"Who?" Marian stilled as Anne placed a thin linen and silk veil over her head and pinned it into place, allowing only some hair to show.

"Sir Guy." The maid wrapped the fabric around her neck and draped it gently over her shoulders, allowing the air to flow freely while hiding the bandage. "Did you run him through and leave him on the side of the road?"

"Of course not." Marian slid her sheathed dagger into a pocket hidden in the folds of her skirt. "I rendered him unconscious and tied him up." A smile touched her lips again. "His men will find him easily enough."

Anne tutted again, shaking her head in disapproval.

Guilt settled around Marian's heart. Had she been cruel? After a long moment, she concluded it had been the kindest of the options afforded her.

A soft knock echoed through the chamber. Anne opened the door.

"My lady." A page bowed low. "Lord de Bough has come and wishes to speak with you directly."

"I shall be down in a moment. Please show him to the garden."

After the page left, Marian took several steadying breaths. While she appeared outwardly collected, chaos reigned inside. With no rest or sustenance, she could not endure much beyond a few moments with the lord. His presence was no burden, yet she found she had little tolerance for company due to the night's events.

"Anne, please prepare a small repass in the great hall. I am famished."

"At once, my lady." With a curtsy, the maid left her chamber.

Marian managed to gather her wits as she made her way through the corridors and down the stairs to the garden. Her mother had planted this small area with flowers and herbs. Roses climbed the arched entrance, and she inhaled their sweet scent as she passed beneath them.

"My lady." Lord de Bough bowed. His charming smile warmed her. "I trust you are well this fine day?"

"I am, my lord." She clasped her hands in front of her. "To what do I owe the pleasure of your company this lovely morning?"

His expression sobered as he pushed a hand through his golden hair. "I have heard rumors, whispers of outlaws targeting outlying farms amidst the terrible destruction caused by the reivers." He pressed his hand to his chest. "I came to see if there is anything I can do to help."

"How kind of you, my lord." Marian walked along a path through the garden. He fell into step beside her. "But I believe we have things well in hand. The Grim Knight has made his presence known."

"Ah, yes." Graham nodded thoughtfully. "Such an intimidating knight will surely make an impression on all who dare cross him. Should you need further assistance, I will provide any men and supplies you need."

"I thank you, my lord. Truly."

"My offer still stands, Mistress Marian."

Her heart thundered in her chest. She swayed, weak with exhaustion. He gripped her elbow to steady her.

"One word from you, and I will summon the bishop. We could be married within a fortnight." His tone softened. "On my honor, I wish only to protect you, good lady. To see you struggle torments me."

"Your offer is kind and more than generous, my lord." She drew away, putting distance between them, her gaze lingering on the rose-covered exit. "I shall take it into consideration, but I must speak with my father before I make any decisions."

"Of course." He followed her out of the garden, coming up beside her as they strode to the stables, where a page stood holding his mount.

"May God grant you mercy, my lord." Marian dipped into a curtsy.

Graham took her hand and pressed a kiss to it. "I shall await your summons, Mistress Marian."

She watched, stoic, as he mounted his horse. When he exited the keep, she exhaled in relief. Her stomach growled a protest at being ignored for so long. She pressed a hand to her middle and turned, heading for the great hall and food.

A shout echoed behind her.

Marian spun toward the sound of hoofbeats and bellowed orders. A small group of soldiers was returning.

Her gaze narrowed on only the rider in the middle. Sir Guy, covered in dirt, hair mussed, eyes wild. He looked positively murderous. She studied him, assessing him for injuries she had not inflicted.

As if sensing her curiosity, he pivoted to face her. Holding her gaze, he slid from the horse's back.

Marian tilted her chin up and turned, leaving him and the chaos of his arrival in her wake.

Inside the great hall, she gathered the morsels Anne had prepared and carried them to her chamber. The last thing she desired at the moment was a confrontation with Sir Guy. Unable to open the door to her chamber, she set her bounty on a table and reached for the handle.

"Mistress Marian." His voice rumbled, low and menacing, behind her.

Curse him.

Taking a deep breath, she greeted him. "Sir Guy. You have returned." Her gaze drifted over his distressed form, and she widened her eyes with feigned concern. "Were you attacked?"

"In a manner." He closed the distance between them.

She pressed her back against her door, reminded of the last time he'd put her in such a position. Her heart pounded and her head felt light. His intense gaze pinned her in place, as though searching for something inside her mind.

"Are…you well?" Marian cleared her throat.

He merely growled in response.

"You look absolutely horrid. Perhaps you should take a hot bath and eat. It might improve your mood."

Her smile and her teasing did not improve his mood. His

eyes narrowed, and she swallowed hard, unable to endure his silent scrutiny.

"My maid has a delightful herbal tea that could soothe your temper." She turned, but he grabbed her wrist and spun her to face him. She stumbled at the motion and grabbed his arms to steady herself.

He hissed in pain, grinding his teeth. Agony flashed in his eyes, brief and clear. She pulled her hand away, realizing her mistake. Her fingers were covered in blood.

She met his gaze. "You are injured?"

"'Tis but a scratch." He stepped back.

"Let me—"

"I do not require false concern for my well-being, my lady." With those words, he strode the short distance to his own chamber, leaving her in stunned silence.

The echo of his slamming door shook the timbers above her head. She flinched and closed her eyes.

Sir Guy was no fool.

What would he do when he uncovered her duplicity? 'Twas only a matter of time. The Grim Knight showed no mercy. Everyone knew it. She would be no exception.

Her fingertips grazed the bandage hidden by her veil. His wrath would come down like an axe upon her neck.

Guilt twisted her conscience, and with a sigh, Marian retrieved the herbal remedies Anne had used earlier.

Chapter Eight

Guy leaned against the back of the tub, his injured arm draped over the side. The scalding water soothed his aching muscles.

He sank beneath the water, allowing it to wash away dirt and mud. Breaking the surface again, he sighed and wiped the water from his eyes. A flash of movement near the door caught his attention.

"Leave it and get out," he growled at the servant.

"If you wish to allow your wound to fester, may your death be on your own head."

Guy twisted, sloshing water over the edge of the bath. Marian stood in the doorway, her arms laden with a small bundle. She arched a brow at him. Even with a wimple covering her head, she could not be mistaken for a demure lady.

"Have you come to drown me?" He sank back into the water, wincing at the pressure on his wound.

"Tempting as that may be, I have come to dress your wound." She cocked her head. "Unless you would rather I leave."

I would rather you join me. The thought crossed his mind unbidden, making his cock stiffen. He closed his eyes and focused on anything but this temptation standing in his chamber.

"Do you know how?" he asked.

Her soft footfalls stopped near the tub. If she dared to glance beneath the water, she would see just how much her presence stirred him. But her gaze remained focused on his face as she pulled a stool close and sat upon it.

He winced as she grasped his arm and unbandaged it, turning the gash toward her. Blood ran down his arm and dripped to the floor.

His gaze remained fixed upon her face. She drew her lower lip between her teeth as she reached for the bundle on the floor.

Using a cloth and a small bucket of warm water near the tub, she cleaned the wound.

He grimaced at the sting.

"I see this is not your first?" Marian's soft voice broke the tension.

His brows drew together. "What do you mean?"

"The wound." She gestured to the scars on his shoulder and then to the few across his torso above the water. "You have quite a collection."

"There are others. On my back. My legs. One injury damn near took off my—" He choked on the word, remembering his place.

A soft smile curved her lips as she threaded a needle. "I expect no less of the Grim Knight."

He hissed at the first poke of the needle and wished for something strong to dull the pain. Instead, he bore it, biting back the curse on his tongue, as she closed the wound. When she finished the final stitch and covered it with soothing herbs, the sting eased to a pulsing awareness.

"You did not have to do that." He shifted as she wrapped a clean cloth around his arm.

"And miss the opportunity to torture you?" She tutted. "Never."

"'Twas a mere flesh wound, compared to others."

"Aye. One requiring seven stitches and a poultice." She released his arm, and he frowned at the loss of her touch. "Keep watch over it. I have seen a scratch kill a grown man."

Guy smirked. "Would you be loath to see me bested by it?"

"'Twould be a fitting end, I should say." Humor flashed in her eyes. As she rose, her gaze drifted, and a blush stole across her cheeks. Without a word, she retrieved her bundle and turned away.

She paused with her hand on the door and glanced over her shoulder. "I cannot have you die yet."

With that parting blow, she exited his chamber, closing the door behind her.

Guy grinned as he sank beneath the water once more.

Thoroughly clean, he rose and dried himself. Pain shot down his arm when he moved it.

He cursed, swallowing the pain along with the shame of being bested by a woman. What rankled him was not the injury itself, but the way in which he'd received it and how the mysterious outlaw managed to outwit him.

The bandit had proved to be an exceptional swordsman. And if those arrows had missed him intentionally, as he suspected, then she was also skilled with a bow. An interesting combination.

Later that evening, Guy sat at the end of the table, a cup of wine clenched in his fist, surveying those in attendance. The ache in his arm subsided as he drank, and his memory replayed not only the events of the night before, but Marian's unexpected kindness. What had prompted it? His mood grew darker and more pensive with every passing moment.

Guy drank deeply from his cup, ignoring the suckling pig and fresh bread on a plate before him. His thoughts returned to the encounter in the forest. There must be a way to find her. If she was part of the band of outlaws stealing from the baron's people, he could uncover their location by following her.

If he knew her identity. Curse the wench for besting him.

His gaze drifted over those in the great hall, his men and the baron's household. Ravenwood sat at the head table, his pale skin glowing in the flickering candlelight. His health had not improved, but he found strength to sit among those who relied upon his leadership. A well-loved and honorable man.

There were blessed few of those among Guy's acquaintance. Even his own conscience was tarnished by past misdeeds, leaving his reputation stained beyond repair. 'Twas of no consequence. The opinions of nobles and peasants alike mattered little.

And yet, knowing Mistress Marian held him in contempt burned at the small remaining piece of his conscience.

He searched for her in the crowd, but she remained absent.

He stabbed a piece of pork with his knife and lifted it to his lips, the small bite igniting his hunger. He set aside his wine and leaned forward to devour the food before him.

A flash of flowing movement drew his attention from his meal. Mistress Marian strode into the room, drifting in a cloud of elegance, wearing a dark red gown with a simple white veil covering her hair.

His gaze narrowed as she approached her father and bent to kiss his head.

Earlier, when he'd returned from the forest, he had caught sight of her across the bailey. There had been no other drive than to go to her. He could not fathom why. She had been wearing the veil then, too, and again when he cornered her outside her chamber.

Since their arrival at the keep, she had worn her hair unbound and bare. Why the sudden desire to cover herself?

Had his teasing remarks made her uncomfortable? The reasoning seemed sound, considering she kept her distance from him whenever possible. Perhaps she loathed him enough to forgo all pretense of polite behavior and ignore him completely.

She laughed, her face brightening with the action. He admired the flash of even white teeth and the sparkle in her hazel eyes, even from this distance. The sound carried through the hall, tinkling like church bells over the village near his childhood home. He shifted in his seat as an inexplicable pull drew him to her.

In all his years, he had never felt anything as strong as this, as if an invisible thread bound them together, slowly winding tighter with every passing hour. He scoffed at the fanciful notion. She was merely a pretty face, with wit and passion to match. Something fresh, a newly polished gem.

She kissed her father again and retreated the way she had come.

Guy swallowed the remaining wine in his goblet and pushed away from the table. With long strides, he followed her, hoping to unravel her secrets. Such a distraction would soothe his aching pride until he could venture back into the woods after dark.

When he reached the long corridor, he paused, waiting for her to move from sight before continuing. The flash of her red skirts belied her direction, and he stalked closer, careful to stay quiet as he crept along the stone passage.

When he reached the far end of the deserted hall, he paused at the sound of quiet conversation. He stood still, waiting, willing his heart to stop lest it give him away.

"Tell them I cannot come this eve. 'Tis too dangerous." Mistress Marian's hushed whisper filled the silence.

"What of the plan?" her companion asked.

"We shall have to delay a few nights." She sighed. "After his encounter in the forest last eve, the Grim Knight is determined to find his attacker."

"There must be another way."

"If we continue on this path, we must ensure his attention remains on the reivers and away from our band of merry men."

"There are whispers, my lady…rumors of the reivers being in league with the neighboring lords."

"Could such a thing be accurate?" Mistress Marian swore. "If there is truth to this, we must uncover it."

The implications of her whispered conversation sank into his mind. The bandit he encountered in the forest had been a woman. She never spoke, but it had been as apparent as the sun crossing the sky. Was the outlaw Mistress Marian? It could not be so…could it?

Perhaps that had been the reason the outlaw remained silent, to conceal her identity. She knew it was *him* in the forest.

A smile crossed his lips at the thought of the veil. It hid the wound he had inflicted; he would wager any amount on it.

The rumors they spoke of, however, required close inspection. With renewed determination and a target for investigation, he slowly backed away, retreating the way he had come.

He slipped down the corridor and quietly entered his chambers. Once inside, he leaned against the door.

"I have you now, my lady."

The events came together in his mind. She had recognized him and hid, hoping he would pass by. When her horse bolted, she fired warning shots in an attempt to scare him away. Instead, he had pursued the threat and forced her to fight.

His blood heated at the memory. Had he known it was her while they fought, he would have drawn it out, savored the moment. Teased her until she lashed out with pure hatred.

Even in their encounter that morning, her wild expression, the pure hatred in her eyes, the way she dug her fingers into his wound…she wanted nothing more than to bring him harm. But why did she come to his chamber and tend to the wound herself? Had guilt driven her to action? Or was there something more beneath the barbs and hatred?

Mistress Marian could have killed him. Twice. And she had let him live. Why allow him to breathe if she abhorred him with such vehemence?

He chuckled even as the fury of her deception pulsed through him. This dichotomy only made him want her more, his simmering desire transformed into molten need.

Guy longed to bask in her fierce wild nature. He wanted nothing more than to defile her perfect image and plunder her false innocence. She was no meek and mild maiden, but a warrior trapped within the confines of society's expectations. He saw beneath the facade she wore with righteous honor. It protected her, but not from him.

He would claim her…all of her. For his own selfish desires.

Retrieving his cloak, he ventured to the stables. Fortunately, his stallion had returned unharmed before him. After the sun set, Guy pulled himself into the saddle and reigned Nix toward the gate.

Now that he knew of Marian's nocturnal adventures, he could track her. It would only be a matter of time before he would uncover the secret meeting location and arrest the bandits involved in her plot.

As he rode toward the village, his mind churned with questions. What gain could she hope for by joining a band of outlaws? Such actions left her vulnerable to attack or injury. Surely, her father would command her to cease if he knew of her actions.

Guy needed to form a plan. He required more information.

More time.

As much as it pained him to throttle his desire to confront her, it would benefit him to be patient. To watch, to observe as a predator would his prey.

Marian would be his. One way or another.

Chapter Nine

Something was amiss. Since the day she had first crossed his path in the king's court, Sir Guy had been a persistent, unavoidable, vexing shadow hovering over her. She had become accustomed to his irritating presence. His almost vulgar provocations had left an impression upon her. So much so, their sudden absence drove her concern for his well-being.

The thought was nearly laughable. Why should she care what happens to the Grim Knight, whose selfish behavior bordered on discourteous—nay, uncouth—especially as a knight of the realm?

She lingered in the doorway, watching the garrison soldiers milling about in small groups. Some training, others observing. There was no sign of their leader, only the captain. Sir Guy's conspicuous absence made her nervous, and her curiosity ran rampant.

Perhaps she had been wrong to go to him in his chambers to tend his wound, but her guilt had guided her action. Seeing him in the bath, completely bare, his body littered with scars old and new, left her unsteady. Such scars were the result of conflict and rage. If the stories of his exploits were based on truth, his past was wrought with agonizing pain.

Seeing him in such a vulnerable state led her to question many things. But it did not change the facts. If he discovered her band of men, he would show no mercy.

Fear gripped her. *Had* he uncovered information concerning her small group of outlaws? She chewed her lip. Marian had not gone into the forest since the night she crossed blades with Sir Guy. She had warned her men, while assuring them of their safety, that their plans would need to be postponed until Sir Guy found quarry elsewhere.

Her plan had worked, in a manner. It had directed scrutiny

to the neighboring lords. The soldiers spoke in hushed tones of both Lord Hayworth and Lord de Bough and the distinct lack of violence in their lands when compared to her father's. Almost as though the reivers targeted them specifically. She could not fathom their reason for doing so.

The stablemaster, Vernon, mentioned Sir Guy's early departure when she visited that morning. He had left before dawn, riding east…or so Vernon claimed. It was now well into the afternoon, and the sun was low on the western horizon.

Four days had passed since their encounter with nary a word or glance from the Grim Knight. Aye, something was surely amiss. She would draw the truth from him when he returned.

Determined, Marian retreated to the keep. She smiled at the servants as she made for her father's chambers. When she reached his door, she knocked softly.

"Enter." His voice came clear enough through the wood but was followed by a hacking cough.

"Father," she said, opening the door. Concern washed over her at the sight of him still abed, pale and listless. "You should have called for me."

"'Tis nothing, daughter." He beckoned for her to come close and patted the bed beside him.

She sat with a sigh and took his frail hand in her own. "You are ill. 'Tis not *nothing*."

"It comes and goes as it pleases." His weak smile gave her hope. "When the weakness strikes, I remain in bed. 'Tis the way of things."

"Have you tried the tea Anne made for you?"

"It smells horrid and tastes bitter." He grimaced at her suggestion. "I would prefer to drink horse piss."

"That means the medicine is working, Father." Marian chuckled at his melodramatic reaction. "You must give it a chance."

He squeezed her hand and sighed, resting his head on the cushions propping him up. "Must I?"

"Aye, Father. You must. For me." Her heart clenched at the thought of losing him, of being alone. "We must improve your health. I require your guidance on all matters."

"If you would marry, you would no longer require my guidance." His bushy brows drew together in mock scorn.

She turned away and grimaced. When she looked back at him, she smiled sweetly. "And who would you recommend I marry? Hmm? One of the feckless sons of a lord at court?"

He scoffed. "There is not a man among them who would properly care for these lands. Nay, it would be wiser to marry someone whose blood runs thick in these parts, who cares for the people along the border."

Marian stared at his careworn face, waiting for him to continue. It was as it had always been, his melancholy moods pushing these conversations. He longed for her to be cared for, loved, protected. And yet, his choice of husband could not have been less reassuring.

"Have you reconsidered Lord de Bough's proposal?" Her father nudged, pulling her from her thoughts. "He would make a fine husband. Combining our two holdings would strengthen our position on the border. Then the king might send a larger garrison to deal with the reivers."

"I spoke with Lord de Bough a few days ago, Father." At his mention of the ongoing conflict, Marian seized the opportunity to direct the conversation away from her marriage. "His lands have not been affected by the reivers as ours have. And Lord Hayworth has not had any attacks on his land in more than a year."

"They should consider themselves fortunate." He coughed and motioned for the goblet of spiced wine.

Marian helped him drink, then placed the goblet on the table beside the bed. She smoothed her hands on her skirts, ignoring their trembling.

"Does it not seem odd?" She licked her lips and pressed forward. "All the attacks over the last year affected none but those under your care?"

"'Tis misfortune indeed, but with the Grim Knight with us, the attacks have ceased." He grinned. "That alone is a blessing."

"These reiver attacks are concentrated solely on *your* lands,

Father." She ignored his praise of Sir Guy and the fact that there had been no attacks since his arrival. "These savages ignore Lord Hayworth and Lord de Bough's lands, as though a wall protects them from brutality."

"My dear, both lords have soldiers to defend their lands. 'Twould be a slaughter should the reivers target their lands as well as mine." He hung his head. "My attentions have never been on building a strong defense but on ensuring those in my care are provided for. The lean years have driven me to make careful decisions concerning the expense for soldiers."

"I understand, Father." Marian took his hand once more. "All will be well."

The conversation had diminished the little strength her father possessed. She saw the ache in him, at his inability to provide everything needed to ensure the best possible outcome for everything and everybody. And yet, his illness aged him, drained what remained of his determined spirit.

Marian soothed him with memories of her mother and her exploits as a child. He laughed, the tension easing from his shoulders as he listened. She sang until his eyes closed and he slept peacefully.

She slipped quietly from the room, instructing the servants to let him rest.

The constriction around her heart tightened. The little hope she had was slipping away like sunlight with approaching darkness. She cursed her inability to act, to do what needed to be done. If it was not her sex that restrained her, it was the threat of being caught. It was only a matter of time before her band of merry men would be uncovered.

Wisdom demanded she disband them and burn her hood.

But one last run would ensure their success. She felt it in her bones.

After dark, she would sneak out of the keep to meet with Samuel and the others. They would finish this mission and part ways.

With renewed vigor, Marian retreated to the stables with instructions for the stable boy to have her mount saddled and ready for her to leave once the sun set.

Purpose filled her as she strode from the stables. Her mind spun with plans for this outing. She only hoped Sir Guy and his men remained in the keep…should he return before nightfall. Perhaps she could entice them to stay with a show of good faith, a reward for their hard work. A few kegs of ale should keep them distracted until morning.

Her father's steward, Randall, stood near the garrison barracks, speaking with the captain. She approached them with a smile.

"Good evening, my lady." Randall bowed. "Is there something you require?"

"Not at all." She turned to the captain, who also bowed. "These good men deserve a small indulgence for all their hard work."

"My lady, you are kind, but—"

She silenced the captain with a wave of her hand. "Nonsense. You and your men have been diligent in your duties. 'Tis my pleasure to reward honorable service."

"Gramercy, Mistress Marian." The captain met her gaze.

"How does a few kegs of ale sound? A small token of my gratitude and an opportunity for your men to rest from their burdens." She turned to Randall. "Have them brought up from the cellars, if you please."

"At once, my lady." Randall took his leave without further prompting.

"Now." Marian turned to survey the people roaming the bailey. "Where is your leader? The fearless Grim Knight?"

"He is elsewhere engaged, my lady." The captain eyed her carefully. "Would you like me to inform you of his return?"

"That will not be necessary." She tugged at the veil covering her neck. "I pray you, enjoy the ale and the evening of rest."

"You are as gracious and kind as people say." He bowed. "As well as beautiful."

As he rose, his eyes glittered with gentle interest. Marian warmed at the compliment.

"My thanks, sir."

"William." A smile played on his lips.

"You flatter me, Captain William." Under his attention, she was very aware of their audience.

The gate burst open behind them, and the Grim Knight came through atop his black destrier. His gaze fixed on Marian with the captain, and his eyes narrowed.

Heat burned through her, warming her face and igniting embers of hate nestled in the pit of her stomach. She ignored his presence and turned back to the gentle captain.

Captain William's expression had tightened with the return of the cursed knight. He bowed to her again. "I bid you good eve, my lady."

Irritation pulsed through her. Must Sir Guy ruin everything with his insufferable presence? She entered the great hall, turning her back on him as he dismounted the beast.

For days, she had believed herself free. And yet, at this one moment, a small wordless exchange left her as furious as if she had confronted him with blades and come to blows.

Memories of their encounter in the forest had her itching for the weight of a blade in her hand. She relished all opportunities to spar with any willing opponent. But her desire to keep her skills a secret limited her ability to practice with as often as she would like.

Inside the great hall, she lingered with the servants as they prepared the hall for the evening meal. Her father had requested to take his dinner in his chambers. It was for the best, considering the state in which she'd found him earlier that day. He needed rest.

She, however, required exertion. Perhaps Samuel would train with her later. She craved the rush of blood pounding through her, the simple determined focus of defeating an opponent.

"Mistress Marian." Her name echoed through the hall. She turned to see the scowling face of her enemy as he strode toward her. "A word?"

She stood tall and braced herself for his lashing. Whatever bee found its way under his armor, she would cope with the irate badger. "Sir Guy." She clasped her hands before her as he approached.

When he reached her, he snatched her wrist and pulled her from the room. She winced at the pressure of his grip. He dragged her down the corridor until they reached a quiet, shadowed alcove. He released her with a shove, placing himself firmly in front of her, blocking her only exit.

Before she could protest, he leaned close, crowding her space further. The scent of leather, horses, and forest drifted around her. Beneath it all, she recognized the scent of his skin, the aroma belonging to him alone. She held her breath in an effort to keep her wits about her.

"You dare allow my men to get drunk on ale with a foe waiting to discover our weakness?" His gaze bore into hers.

She licked her lips. "I merely wished to reward their service."

"They have done nothing to earn it." He braced one hand on the wall beside her head and studied her carefully.

Marian swallowed under his intense scrutiny. Her mind raged against his brutish actions, but her limbs did not listen. Her arms hung, useless, at her sides. Her legs remained locked in place. There was nowhere to go where he could not capture and confront her.

A wicked smile curved his sensual lips. His eyes darkened in the shadows. "Unless you wish to distract them…to keep them inside the keep?"

"Why would I want such a thing?" she asked, her mouth dry.

"I know you better than you think I do, Marian."

His breath caressed her cheek. The sound of her name on his lips twisted her insides into a molten puddle of heat.

"You know nothing of me," she hissed.

Sir Guy lifted a gloved hand and removed the leather from his hand. Her breath caught. His long, calloused fingers drifted close, brushing her cheek, teasing beneath the fabric of the veil, following the line of her jaw. Embers sparked beneath his touch and radiated through her.

She fought the desire igniting inside her, cursed her weak body for rebelling against her restraint. It refused to retreat from his touch. Instead, her body basked in his soft attention as he trailed his fingers lower and lower.

He traced her jaw, toying with the hem of the fabric tickling her throat. His blunt thumb brushed the fullness of her lower lip.

"I know passion dwells deep inside you," he whispered, his touch becoming pure torment. "Such fire should not be hidden from the world."

He gently tugged the fabric, loosening it from the pins holding it in place. As it slid across her cheek, panic plunged into her chest, stilling her heart. The veil fell free, exposing the smooth column of her neck…and the red, puckered scar along her throat.

"Mistress Marian…" His fingertips brushed the scar. "Where did you get this?"

She winced. Not from pain or disgust at his touch, but from his unspoken promise of retribution. Words failed her. Not a sound came to her lips. No defense. No curse. Nothing would counter the accusation in his heated gaze.

"Have you nothing to confess?" He traced his fingers along her throat until they reached the hem of her gown.

Steadfast, she held her ground. She would make no confession. He could not drag it from her, even if he tortured her.

"I have unraveled your secret, vixen." He murmured, his voice low and even. "Your skills with a blade, with a bow. Your little band of outlaws."

Her gaze narrowed, her lips thinning, a response in itself. She cursed herself for reacting. Fear skittered along her spine. "What have you done with them?"

"Nothing." A wolfish grin curved his devilish mouth. "Yet."

Hope flared in her breast, but he was the Grim Knight. His past, if it were even half as bloody and horrid as the stories claimed, as his scars showed, promised one thing—he would not hesitate to act should he deem it necessary. Somehow, she had to convince him of her men's innocence before it was too late.

"What do you want from me?" she asked.

His leer sent a shiver down her spine.

"First, I require the truth. From your lips. Give me that, and I shall consider payment for my silence."

Saints preserve me.

But no amount of prayer would save her. Not with the Grim Knight holding her life in the balance.

Chapter Ten

The hard line of her lips parted, and her eyes widened.

Check.

Guy disliked games, especially chess, but he had a talent for strategy. He stood firm, knowing if he budged even a fraction, if he showed any route of escape, she would grasp the opportunity to flee. He had carefully positioned his pieces and was slowly encircling her.

Her soft breaths quickened, and he leaned against the wall, holding her in place. He pinned her with a level gaze.

Mine, a possessive voice whispered deep inside him.

"I speak the truth." She licked her lips. "I have done nothing to warrant an inquisition."

Such evasive answers should have gnawed at his patience…and yet, he savored the dance.

He had missed it these past few days, this verbal sparring. What would she do with a blade in her hand? With the opportunity to plunge a dagger deep into his heart? Would she dare follow through with what she did not in the forest?

"Very well, vixen." He reached to the sheath on his hip and withdrew his own dagger. Tilting the hilt in her direction, he held it steady. "Take it."

Fear flared in her wide eyes before they narrowed with distaste. "And what do you think I will do? Run you through? End your miserable life?" She cocked her head. "Is that what you *wish*? I will not be drawn out in such a manner."

"Surely, you have imagined it?" He inhaled deeply, letting her delicate but dangerous allure surround him. Consume him.

"Imagined what? Killing you?" Her fingers traced the hilt. "A thousand times, each more gruesome than the last."

"Lies." He chuckled at her brazenness.

"You asked for truth, and I have given it. 'Tis no concern

of mine if you cannot stomach it."

"Had you wanted to kill me, you would have done so in the forest, under cover of darkness when you had me bound and at your mercy." He dropped the dagger to his side, turning it so the hilt fit his palm.

"Whoever had you thus should have finished what they started and saved me this conversation." She held her ground, determination and strength clear in her stance, but he saw cracks form in her icy demeanor.

"Come now, vixen. Admit it. You bested me in the woods, brought me to my knees." He drew his tongue across his teeth. "Such a feat is hard-won. There is no one to overhear your confession. How did it feel to draw my blood under that hood of anonymity? An advantage, to be sure, but your delightful attributes are difficult to hide."

Her jaw worked, flexing with the pressure of irritation. Every well-aimed barb struck, blow after blow, chipping away her restraint. Her lies, he would expose them all. Expose her. One way or another.

"It took a little time to recognize the truth." He tugged the thread unraveling her. "I cannot believe I did not see it more quickly, but it seemed ridiculous to imagine the baron's daughter dressed in black, running with a pack of thieves in the dead of night while reivers plague the land."

Every one of her breaths was measured and deep. Still, she did not break.

"What would your father say of your reckless behavior?"

A hitch in her breath betrayed her more than any spoken confession could. Stubborn vixen.

"Perhaps I should tell him of the bandit I encountered in the forest?" He savored the horror in her expressive eyes. "Would you lie to your ailing father as you lie to me?"

When tears spilled silently down her cheeks, she finally dropped her gaze. "Damn you."

Checkmate.

When she met his gaze again, fire flicked in the hazel depths of her eyes.

"What do you want from me?" She repeated the question, but this time defeat rang through her tone.

"Surrender."

She scoffed. "You would have me lay down my weapons and admit defeat?"

"Absolutely not."

"Then…what?"

"Tell me the truth." He eased back, giving her space, and tucked his dagger back into its sheath. "Why put yourself in danger? Taking on the cowl of an outlaw certainly makes you a target for the reivers."

She heaved a deep breath. "That is exactly why I do it."

"You *choose* to put yourselves in the path of the reivers?" He laughed, the sound low. "If you want to suffer a horrible death, I can save you the trouble."

"There is something amiss. The neighboring lords have had no attacks—not from bandits, not reivers. Nothing. Their lands remain untouched while my father's holdings burn to the ground."

He silently pondered her observation for a moment, considering the possibilities. When he had first arrived and surveyed the damage, he saw only the carnage left by the reivers. After a few nights of wandering the region, venturing into neighboring territories, his discoveries aligned with her theory.

"You believe it is an orchestrated effort to target your father's lands?" he asked, stroking his jaw.

"I *know* it is."

"Have you any proof?"

"None." She frowned. "But there have been whispers…"

"Whispers do nothing to back your assertion, Mistress Marian." He inhaled deeply, resigning himself to the course before them. "If we are to unravel these mysteries, we must have solid evidence of the treachery."

"Exactly what I was doing before you thrust yourself into the middle of my plans."

"Why ask for help from the king if you had things well in hand?" He sneered.

"It was my father's request, not mine. I hoped you and your men would focus your attention on the reivers while we uncovered who was behind the coordination of these attacks."

If looks could kill, hers would have set him ablaze. Her spirit enflamed his desire tenfold.

"All you had to do was ask, my lady."

"And would you have acquiesced so willingly?"

Guy closed the distance between them, pressing his body to hers, pinning her to the wall. Cold dug into his palm where it rested against the stone.

Her eyes flew wide, flickering between his own eyes and his lips. When her breath caught, he seized his opportunity.

"Aye, I would." He tilted his head, eyeing her mouth with hunger. "For a price."

"I am no whore, sir."

"I never assumed you were." He lost himself in her. "You require my aid and possess something I desire. It seems a fair bargain."

"There is nothing fair about what you ask of me."

"I have not yet told you what I ask."

"I can imagine the thoughts crossing your deviant mind." She paused. "What do you want?"

"Your surrender."

"We have already established that."

"You misunderstand me, vixen." He laughed before growing serious again. "I want your total and complete surrender. You in my bed. At my mercy."

Her throat worked. Panic and desire painted her skin. "For how long?"

"Indefinitely."

"My father will never allow it."

"We shall see, vixen."

Mistress Marian straightened, the action bringing their lips dangerously close. He longed to taste her, to seal their bargain with a kiss, but he waited, watching her, his heart thundering in his chest.

"If I agree, you will help me uncover this plot?"

"On my honor." A wicked smile curved his lips.

"You have no honor."

He could not refute it.

"When must I provide an answer?"

"I shall give you until the morrow, when the sun reaches its highest point in the sky."

"Very well. You shall have my answer then."

Disappointment filled him as he stepped back. The spell between them snapped. So strong was his desire to capture her lips, to take what he wanted from her supple body, to draw out both of their pleasures. But he could wait. 'Twas only a matter of time, then she would be his.

"Good eve, my lady." He inclined his head and pivoted, stalking down the hall.

He would join his men in their revelry, but his heart twisted at the thought of Mistress Marian alone thinking of his offer. He had lain himself bare, but she too exposed herself…and her desires.

Guy knew sleep would not come easily tonight. He intended to drink himself into a stupor and pray she came to her senses.

Chapter Eleven

Staring at the flickering flames in the hearth, Marian contemplated the devil's bargain. The Grim Knight knew everything…as though he ripped away a layer of her life, stripping her bare, leaving her exposed to criticism. When he peeled away the veil covering the wound he'd inflicted, her heart had stopped. His dark gaze haunted her as it dropped to the tender scar, still red with healing ointment.

Recognition had flashed in his eyes, followed by triumph. Even though he uncovered her secret, she would not give him the benefit of hearing her confess her deeds. If he bound and tortured her, she would not give him the satisfaction.

She paced the floor in only her shift, the stifling warmth of the fire agitating her further. She crossed to the window and opened it. A cool breeze drifted in, the night air soothing her skin. Her gaze searched the night sky, as if it would give the solution to her problem.

A problem she alone created. *Curses.*

In the distance, she heard the revelry of the soldiers. Her distraction worked, but her desire to leave the keep had vanished the moment Sir Guy cornered her in the hallway. He would follow her if she dared to leave. Instead, she shut herself in her chamber, drinking wine and cursing herself a fool for believing she could outwit him.

Damn the insufferable man.

The whispers had been true. Even with his ruthless reputation, he had proven quite thorough and steadfast in his duties. He saw everything with eyes sharp as a hawk's and a conscience unbothered by bloodshed.

If he had known who was beneath the hood that night, would he have shown mercy had he gained the upper hand? She shivered at the prospect. It could have ended with a sword in her gut. She had been fortunate to escape with a meager scratch. Now that he knew the truth, he would never again allow her the freedom to leave alone. She would know no peace with him here.

Even if she managed to evade his watchful eye, he would go to her father and reveal it all.

Fear gripped her heart and squeezed. Such a revelation would force her father's hand. He would marry her to the closest eligible lord. The horror struck her like a physical blow. She leaned against the stone wall and inhaled deeply, wishing she were anywhere but trapped in this chamber. In this keep.

But the alternative left her breathless and shaking.

The Grim Knight's bargain.

Could she truly sell her soul, her body, to protect herself? To protect her people?

His offer rang, clear and sharp, in her memory. Marian pressed a hand to her stomach as it twisted. How could she possibly contemplate this offer?

'Twas not a proposal of marriage, or even of partnership. It was an exchange of terms. Her compliance in exchange for his.

Her body for his silence.

Her soul for his services.

Sir Guy had little to recommend him. In truth, he represented everything she abhorred. War. Death. Torment. Suffering. His consistent distaste for her company mingled with vulgar flirtation to create a strange dichotomy. 'Twas obvious enough he craved her companionship in his bedchamber, but his behavior toward her constantly undermined whatever attraction she might have harbored for him had he shown a kinder nature.

That he was handsome, there was no doubt. His skills with a sword were unparalleled by any she had ever before seen. Even small glimpses of gentility vanished without a trace when he allowed his inner demons to consume him. They ruled his conscience and ruined his allure.

Marian shifted uncomfortably at the memory of her body's earlier reaction to his presence. He radiated confidence. It warmed her along with his teasing questions. Fear and uncertainty rendered her immobile.

And yet, had she wanted to shove him aside or use his own dagger to castrate him, she could have done so. Why had she not acted?

Thoughts of her father consumed her. If he knew the truth, he would not rest until she was wed and sent away. No longer would she have her forests, her merry band of outlaws, her freedoms. She would be trapped in a union that would render her toothless.

There was not a soul she could run to. No one with whom she could form an alliance to defeat those who threatened her father, his lands, and his people. She did not trust the neighboring lords or the king. They would demand worse from her than the simple arrangement Sir Guy had laid at her feet.

He only asked for surrender. A simple, unadorned transaction.

She could not help but feel her very soul being ripped from her at the prospect.

But there was nothing for it. She had only one solution.

Make a deal with the devil.

Sir Guy had granted her until the following day to give her reply, but sleep would never come until she was assured of his silence and they had officially sealed their bargain.

Forgoing a covering, Marian slipped from the room, her shift loose around her shoulders. She shivered as she crossed the quiet space between their chambers and knocked on his door. Part of her prayed he was abed.

When the door opened, her heart was thundering like a calvary charging into battle. Sir Guy's form filled the narrow space, his brow arched in surprise. Before she could state her purpose, he pushed the door further open and gestured for her to enter.

Wordlessly, she hurried past him. Perhaps this was a mistake, but there would be no retreat. Her decision had been made.

When she turned to face him, he closed the door and leaned against it.

"My lady."

His wolfish grin stoked the panic in her gut.

"To what do I owe the pleasure of your company at this late hour?"

Her gaze drifted across his bare chest. Dark hair dusted the muscled expanse, disappearing beneath the hose slung low on his hips. *Saints.* Strength radiated from him as he rose slowly to his full height.

She watched his muscles shift, sinewy and sleek beneath his skin. Her fingers itched to trail over them, to feel the power harnessed there. Just like the day she had seen him in the bath.

Marian clenched her hands into tight fists and met his amused gaze.

"Do you like what you see?" he asked, his voice rough and husky.

She shook her head. "I have come to tell you my reply."

"It could not wait until morning?" He stalked closer, and she backed away, keeping distance between them.

"I cannot sleep until an agreement is struck." She extended her hand. "I shall offer myself in exchange for your aid in uncovering the reiver's plot."

He reached for her hand, but she pulled it away and finished speaking.

"You will also not mention a word of my past or present actions to my father. Or to any other soul."

"You have my vow." He clasped her hand in his.

Warmth suffused her with the solid weight of his grip.

He pulled her against him. His heat surrounded her, his skin burning through her thin shift. She pressed a hand to his chest. His heart pounded beneath her fingertips. He was hewn from flesh and blood, not stone and ice.

Sir Guy's sharp inhale drew her attention to his face. Hunger simmered in his eyes.

She licked her lips. Even though her mind rioted at the thought of his embrace, the terms of her agreement bound her.

She scratched her nails across the skin covering his heart.

"Marian," he groaned. "You torment me."

"I could say the same." Even to herself, her voice seemed

strained, distant. Uncertain.

"You know nothing of torment, vixen." His eyes glittered in the firelight as his hands settled at her waist.

The gentle pressure singed her. Need pooled in the pit of her stomach, between her thighs.

She studied his face. His hungry green eyes. The aquiline line of his nose, bearing scars and breaks long healed. The faint etchings of wounds from battles carved on his skin. His plush, soft lips curved in pleasure.

Curiosity tugged at her.

Marian traced her fingers along his jaw, feeling rough stubble beneath her touch. His eyes drifted closed, his lips parting with a silent breath.

She marveled at his response. Did she truly have such power over him? A man who could easily take what he wanted, what she had agreed to give him. And yet, he showed restraint. It emboldened her.

His words floated through the haze in her mind. *You torment me.*

Before her senses could return, she rose up and pressed her mouth to his. The simple press of her lips to his sent a bolt of lightning through her body, straight to her core. Her arousal stunned her, but she threw caution to the wind and clung to him, ensuring every part of her pressed against him. *More.* Her mind screamed. *More.*

The Grim Knight melted beneath her kiss. His lips molded to hers, his tongue brushing the seam, seeking entrance. She opened for him, and her abhorrence disintegrated, burning to ash at their feet. Desperate hunger clawed free from deep inside her.

He tightened his grip, the fabric of her shift bunching in his fist. Warm air brushed her inner thighs, now slick with desire.

Guy lifted her, his fingers digging into the flesh where her thighs creased. He carried her three steps to an oversized chair near the fireplace where he sat, cradling her in his lap. He captured her lips again, cupping her jaw in his hand, devouring every moan.

A dying flame burned low in the hearth. Candlelight glowed from the table, casting them in muted shadow. She ran her fingers through his hair. The soft strands teased her palm. She tugged, and he stiffened beneath her.

All of him.

His body tensed as his cock pressed against her hip. He hissed at the pressure as she tipped his head back, forcing him to meet her gaze.

Passion blazed deep within him, an unquenchable flame. She longed to unleash him, to let his fire consume her.

"Sir—"

"Guy," he grunted. His hands remained impassive as he studied her, one resting heavily on her hip, the other cradling her cheek. "Call me by my name, Marian. We are beyond pleasantries, beyond propriety."

"Guy." Part of her shattered with delight when the tension eased from him as his name left her lips. She released his hair, gently sliding her fingers along his stubbled jaw. "Why do you not take what I offer?"

"I have every intention of claiming my prize, vixen." He slowly stood and helped her to her feet before capturing the hem of her shift, gathering it into his fist.

Her breath hitched as he drew the garment over her head. He dropped it onto the chair they'd vacated only moments earlier. She shivered as his gaze raked her naked form.

"Saints preserve me," Guy murmured, placing his hands on her hips and nudging her back until she tumbled onto the bed.

Surprised, she struggled to sit up, but he prowled close, pushing her to the center of the bed, looming just out of reach as he joined her. Her thighs parted as she sank into the bed linens.

Guy's hungry gaze skimmed her breasts, her stomach, to the downy hair between her thighs. A growl ripped from his throat as he lowered himself and kissed her stomach. His peppered kisses trailed down, down, until his lips brushed her mound. He parted her folds and his breath teased her sensitive cunt.

She threaded her fingers in his hair as he licked her. Pleasure sparked through her body. A moan broke free, echoing in the bedchamber. He watched her as he feasted upon her. He lapped at her, devouring the arousal he had created with his kiss, with his touch. When she thought she could no longer take the building pressure, he teased a finger into her, thrusting gently as his tongue tormented her.

Her hands flew to the linens, grasping for purchase. She gathered fistfuls to keep from bucking off the bed.

He pinned her with his weight and persisted, determined to bring her a pleasure beyond anything she had before experienced.

Nothing felt like this. Nothing.

She stifled a shout when the sensations peaked, pushing her into oblivion. Slowly, her body sank back into the bed.

Guy pressed a soft kiss to her trembling cunt before rising to his knees. He stared down at her sated form with a grin on his glistening mouth, a conqueror surveying his prize.

Without a word, he climbed off the bed, retrieved her shift, and put it on the bed. "You should return to your chambers."

"But our bargain?" Marian rose, but wobbled slightly as she sat up so braced herself. "I may be innocent in the ways of the world, but I am not ignorant. Why have you stopped?"

"When I claim you, Marian, I will savor every moment. Each delightful moan. You will cry out my name as I take you. Over and over." His eyes darkened.

She glimpsed the thickness of his cock pressed against the fabric of his hose.

"But that will not be this night."

"Why not?" She snatched the shift and pulled it over her head, aware of his attention upon her nude form, shame settling around her. Clothed, she stood to face him, toe-to-toe. "Have I displeased you?"

"Of course not." With a grimace and a curse, he ran his fingers through his hair. "Marian, listen to me carefully."

She ground her teeth, waiting. Men were fickle creatures, far more so than women. Why did he not want her?

Even after such pleasure, she craved more. If she sold her

soul for this, she would damn well uphold her end of the bargain.

"'Tis almost dawn."

Her attention flickered to the window to see hazy blue painting the starry sky. He took her into his arms, and she stiffened at the contact. His gentle caress along her spine melted her resistance, stroke by stroke. Damn him.

"In a few hours, we ride. If I take my pleasure now, you will be in no state to sit a horse." He tipped up her chin and grinned. "When I finish with you, the last thing you will want is to be in the saddle."

Realization struck her and warmed her cheeks. She shoved him away. "Damn you."

He pulled her close again and pressed a lingering, tender kiss to her lips. "Go rest, vixen."

Marian stumbled from his chambers, her body still humming with the pleasure he gave her. The moment she climbed into her bed, her irritation faded as the sweet bliss of his kiss surrounded her.

Perhaps this bargain had been a blessing.

Devil take them both.

Chapter Twelve

As dawn broke, Guy abandoned any hope of sleep. After the stolen moments of pleasure, he had chased Marian from his chamber lest his resolve crumble to dust.

When he'd offered the bargain in the shadowed corridor, he never expected her to take it. Her pride had been stronger than her fear. Part of him thought she would go directly to her father and expose her own folly rather than accept this offer. He gave her time and a simple ultimatum should she refuse.

In those silent hours before dawn, he prayed he had not revealed his true intentions by pushing the bounds of propriety. When she had come to him wearing only a thin shift, her hair unbound, 'twas as though his prayers were answered.

She tasted like the sweetest honeyed wine mulled with spice. Her kiss warmed him, heated his blood, branded his very soul.

This was what he had craved from the moment he saw her at the king's palace. He'd seen the vibrant passion fluttering beneath her demure expression, a caged bird begging to be free. Her intense dislike for him was the biggest obstacle to overcome.

Still, he did not believe for a moment she'd accepted this bargain because she desired him. He had forced her hand. Unfair to be sure, but there was no other way to show her…to convince her of his sincerity. He burned for her.

Which was exactly why he had given her a taste of pleasure, then shooed her from his presence. He wanted her to crave him with the same burning intensity. If that meant he would need to woo her, he would do so. Even if it meant sacrificing his own comfort and seeking his own relief. But taking himself in hand had done nothing to alleviate the ache. Sleep and blissful release still eluded him.

Instead of chasing that which would not come, he dressed and retreated to the bailey. The soldiers had spent the night drinking until the barrels of ale were empty. He should rouse the lot and order them to train.

Any other day, he would have done so without a second thought…and yet, the idea shattered at the possibility of Marian awaking to find him driving them to exhaustion. She would assume it was punishment for their revelry. She would curse him for a taskmaster and a brute.

He did not see it as a punishment but as an expectation. He had a standard to maintain, and the garrison would live up to it regardless of Mistress Marian's kindness.

He stepped into the early morning air. Servants milled about, bustling with provisions, tending to their duties. His agitation festered into something heated, burning under his skin.

Guy climbed to the top of the walls and walked them, around and around, until the sun was full up. His mind churned with thoughts of Marian and their newly formed alliance. He needed to focus on the task at hand.

There was a plot. The targeted attacks proved one thing for certain—someone was giving very specific orders. Reivers, like those he'd encountered years before, struck without warning, seeking out the weakest victim. They cared not for the politics of landholders and loyalties. They were merciless thieves.

And yet, the neighboring lords weathered no such attacks. Something was certainly amiss and he…*they* would uncover it. Together.

Guy leaned against the stone wall and surveyed the bailey below. The soldiers were starting to stir, slowly filing out of their quarters. He should speak with the captain to arrange a new rotation to survey the baron's lands. So long as the soldiers were present, they deterred attack.

As he made his way down, he spied the captain near the main hall, speaking with a comely maid. The captain snapped to attention when Guy approached. The maid scurried off with only a glance at him.

"Sir Guy," the captain said with a bow.

"Captain, what have you?"

"The evening watch has returned, sir." His quick and

concise report revealed nothing out of the ordinary. They discussed expanding the number of rotations and doubling the men to maintain continued vigilance.

Guy had to admit, Captain William took his position seriously and conducted his duties with painstaking precision. He admired the man's determination and grit. There had been many over the years who took little pride in their position, but this captain put them all to shame.

Being able to trust him, however, was something else entirely.

"Very good, Captain. Proceed." Guy stepped away, looking toward the great hall as the captain retreated to the barracks.

A shout behind him brought his hand to his pommel as he spun to face the gate. He rested his hand on the hilt as a rider in messenger's livery came to a halt, his horse snorting and dancing.

"What is it?" Her voice wrapped around him in a sensual embrace. Guy glanced over his shoulder to find Marian standing in the doorway.

"I bear a message for Lord Ravenwood." The messenger dismounted, strode to her, and bowed low. "My lady, Lord de Bough requests the presence of you and your father. He wishes you to join him in breaking bread to celebrate your success in protecting the border."

Guy ground his teeth, his hand still poised on his sword. They had done nothing but deter further attacks. There had been no battles, no confrontations, not even a sighting of the reivers since they arrived. He scowled at the messenger. What was the pompous lord playing at?

"Lord Hayworth will also be in attendance," the messenger added, offering a sealed parchment to Marian.

"His invitation is most gracious." She accepted the parchment and held it in her fist. "But my father has other plans for this evening."

Guy seized his opportunity and stepped closer, coming beside her. Her body tensed, but she showed no other discomfort at his proximity.

"I would be honored to escort you this evening, should you

wish to attend." Guy bowed. "I am yours to command, my lady."

He lifted his gaze to find her incredulous hazel eyes searching his face, her lips soft and rounded with surprise.

She sobered quickly and turned to face the messenger. "'Twould be an honor. Please inform Lord de Bough we shall be in attendance."

The messenger took his leave, mounted his horse, and turned away. The moment he passed through the gate, Marian spun and returned to the great hall without a word to Guy.

He stalked after her. When he was close enough, he caught her by the wrist. "Marian."

She rounded on him, eyes wide and mouth set. "Not here," she hissed.

He released her and followed her through the great hall. When they reached the small solar, she glanced down the halls, both directions, before closing the door behind him.

"Have you taken leave of your senses?" Marian threw her hands up. "Do you realize what you have done?"

Guy leaned against the door and shrugged, folding his arms across his chest to keep from reaching for her. He ached to kiss her, to make her fall apart in his arms. All in good time.

"Saints preserve me." She pinched the bridge of her nose. "I am surrounded by fools."

"What harm can come from attending a meal?" Guy asked, his tone even.

"Lord de Bough has requested my hand a half dozen times over this past year." She gritted her teeth. "The last occasion no more than a sennight ago."

"And you have refused him?" The mere thought of a feathered pompous ass laying hands on Marian boiled his blood. It grew ever more difficult to refrain from reacting, from betraying how much it truly bothered him, the thought of her marrying another.

"He is not deterred by my refusal." She sighed. "The last time, I said I would consider it."

Guy straightened, dropping his arms to his sides and clenching his hands in fists. "You are *not* considering his proposal." It was not a question. Fury poured through him.

"Of course I am not considering it. But in accepting this invitation, you have placed me in an uncomfortable position." She rubbed her head. "He will most certainly ask again, and I am running out of patience with him."

"Have you told your father?"

"Aye." Marian met his gaze, exhaustion extinguishing the fire in her. "He believes it would be a fine match and encourages it wholeheartedly."

"Fuck." Guy noted the surprise on her face at his use of the word, but he made no move to apologize. They were beyond propriety and expectations.

"Why did you offer to escort me?" she asked, her tone soft as a feather.

"We have a bargain." He grinned, but no humor reached his soul. "I vowed to help uncover the truth. There is something afoul, and I intend to find it. This invitation provides us with an opportunity to search for answers."

"You do not trust Lord de Bough?" Marian studied him.

"I trust no one." He paused, taking in a deep breath. "Do you trust him?"

She shrugged and dropped her gaze.

"If you trusted him, you would have accepted his proposal of marriage." He hooked his finger beneath her chin and lifted it until he could drown himself in her lovely eyes. "Do you trust me?"

Marian scoffed. "Not one wit."

"Good. You should trust no one." His fingertips grazed the curve of her jaw, down her neck, his thumb brushing the developing scar he left with his blade. "Especially me."

"Why?" Her tongue darted out to wet her lips, desire burning beneath the scowl marring her brow.

"I told you. I am not a good man."

"And yet you offered aid?"

"In exchange for surrender." A wicked smile tugged at his lips. "Do you regret it?"

She shook her head and stepped closer, her hand coming to

rest on his chest. His heart pounded at her simple touch.

"Do you think it wise to accompany me this evening?" Her gaze fixed on his mouth. "If Lord de Bough sees us together, he may draw the wrong conclusion."

"Does it matter what he thinks?" He took her waist, drawing her to him. "Let him fester in jealousy."

"Why would we do something so reckless?" she whispered, her breath caressing his jaw.

"Because this is our opportunity to spy on your supposed allies." He rocked his hips against her. "I intend to take full advantage of their hospitality."

"Guy…"

His name on her lips felt like a silken caress.

"If you betray me, I will run you through myself. Do you understand?"

A laugh broke from him. "I expect nothing less, vixen."

She stepped out of his embrace to glare at him. "I vow it on my mother's grave. Do not cross me."

"On my honor."

"You have no honor." She straightened her kirtle and tucked a strand of hair behind her ear. "Now I must speak with my father and inform him of our plans. Ready the horses, I will join you directly."

"At once, my lady." He opened the door and gestured for her to exit ahead of him.

Guy watched as she retreated down the hall. When she disappeared, he shook his head and drew in a deep breath. His cock ached, and he adjusted his hose. Riding would certainly deter these amorous thoughts.

He allowed himself a smile. 'Twas good to know his bargain had not broken her spirit.

As he prepared for their departure, he reevaluated his tactics. The bargain had been a bluff. He would never have exposed her to her father's censure. Such information would have only driven the baron to secure a husband for her.

When she accepted his offer, he came one step closer to obtaining the one thing he wanted more than gold.

More than security.
Guy wanted her for his own.
And he would stop at nothing to ensure success.

Chapter Thirteen

Marian's forced laughter echoed through the great hall, Lord Graham de Bough preening under her attention. Her companion and host had no reason to believe her humor was contrived, even though it physically pained her to be bound by his company during the feast. She was in no mood to play a demure maiden.

When she arrived at his estate, Graham had welcomed her with warmth and kindness, smothering her with compliments. It was almost more than she could bear.

In the past, their interactions had been pleasant. His manners befitted his position, and her father spoke highly of their neighbor. He had been close friends with Graham's parents. When they perished in an accident, Marian's father had come to Graham's aid, offering support and guidance, which strengthened the bond between households. 'Twas not long after that when father expressed interest in joining the two houses in marriage. While Marian could find no fault with Graham, she did not wish to be bartered and traded like a cow, without consideration for her feelings.

Graham had waited, his persistence increasing with each passing year. Their hasty conversation in the garden revealed an earnest demand that left her unsteady. She had only agreed to contemplate the union to silence him, but it seemed her response had instilled hope in the young lord.

He swept her along beside him, giving her a tour of his keep before leading her to the great hall where the guests slowly gathered.

The only saving grace had been the stalwart, brooding presence of Guy as he followed behind them. She prayed he was taking note of their surroundings as her entire focus had been on distracting Graham with inconsequential conversation.

When they took their seats in the great hall, Graham invited her to sit to his right so they might continue a discussion of court affairs. He balked when she told Guy to occupy the empty seat beside her, but he calmed when Guy explained it was Ravenwood's wish he remain by her side to ensure her protection. Graham laughed at the absurdity. No harm would befall her beneath his roof, but he allowed the concession, if only to appease her.

As they dined, Marian picked at her food while she struggled to engage her host. He enjoyed speaking of himself, of his accomplishments. In the past, she had never noticed how preoccupied he seemed with himself. He droned on and on, leaving Marian to wish she were far from this table, from him.

"'Tis distressing to hear your father is unable to leave his chamber due to illness." Graham sipped his wine.

She stiffened at the mention of her father's predicament. No one outside of herself and a handful of servants knew of the downturn in his health. She preferred to keep its severity from becoming gossip among the gentry, lest they take advantage of his weak state.

"On the contrary." Marian smiled, lifting her own goblet. "My father moves quite freely through the keep and grows stronger every day."

"How wonderful." Graham pinned her with a crystal blue gaze, his golden hair glinting in the candlelight. "I hoped he would attend the festivities this evening."

"He sends his regrets, but there were matters demanding his attention." Her simple explanation should deter further question of his health. She disliked lying, but Guy's earlier instructions lingered in her mind. *Trust no one.*

As she drank, she scanned the guests. Out of the corner of her eye, she noted Guy sitting tall beside her, his goblet clenched in his fist, a scowl carved into his handsome face. He looked positively terrifying. Even the servants pointedly avoided him as they served the meal and refilled goblets.

"I cannot tell you how delighted I am to have you attend as my personal guest." Graham said, leaning closer, his voice low. "You look as though you belong here, by my side. Lovely and radiant as a summer sunrise after a long winter."

"You flatter me, my lord." Marian bowed her head, unable to face him. A shiver racked through her. She disliked his amorous attention. Perhaps this evening had been a mistake.

"Have you given any further consideration to my offer?" he asked, clearly admiring her profile.

"I have not." She twisted a goblet between her fingertips, distracted by the glint of metal, wishing it were a dagger. "You must forgive me, my lord. My mind has been occupied of late. The reivers—"

"You need not fear them if you join with me, Mistress Marian." He rested his hand on hers. "Say the word, and I will kill them all myself."

What little food she had eaten roiled in her gut, threatening to come back up. She gently moved her hand from beneath his and pressed her fingertips to her heart, wanting more than anything to remove the memory of his touch from her mind.

"I am moved by your offer, my lord, but I have other commitments I must attend to before I consider marriage. My father needs me, and I cannot abandon him at such a time."

"If we wed, I assure you, both the reivers and your father will be taken care of."

His smile seemed sincere, and yet, she could not suppress the suspicion in her mind.

"You have my word. I will do whatever it takes to ensure you are protected."

"Have they attacked this far east?" she asked, curiosity tugging at her mind, even as she wished desperately to change the topic of discussion. "The reivers?"

"Not in more than a year." Graham cleared his throat and drank deeply from his cup. "I have doubled my soldiers, and they patrol daily to keep things quiet."

"I pray your good fortune continues." Marian finished the wine in her goblet.

"We should return, my lady."

Guy's voice severed the tension pulling between her and Graham, saving her from having to respond further. She looked at him, a grateful smile on her lips. He nodded, not breaking his pensive scowl.

Slowly, she rose from her seat and turned to her host, who also stood.

"I have enjoyed your delightful company, my lady." Graham took her hand and pressed a kiss upon the back. His eyes flashed deep blue as they met hers. "Until next time."

"My thanks for your hospitality, my lord." She withdrew her hand and tucked it in the folds of her skirt.

"Allow me to escort you out." He moved to lead, but Marian blocked his path.

"There is no need to interrupt such a fine celebration on my behalf." She smiled brightly, her face hurting with the effort. "We can manage quite well on our own. Sit. Enjoy your guests. I have occupied too much of your time already."

"You could never occupy too much of my time, Mistress Marian." He bowed low.

Heat flared along her throat and crept into her cheeks. Demurely hiding her face, she stepped past him, heading for the exit. She cared not whether Guy kept pace.

The moment the cool night breeze kissed her face, she inhaled. The stifling air in the great hall combined with Lord Graham's attentions had left her flushed and desperate for peace. She stared at the night sky, admiring the lights scattered across the dark canopy overhead.

"Come." The soft order echoed gruffly behind her as Guy stepped forward, heading for the stables.

While she had not forgotten his presence, his brusque nature unsteadied her. After so many hours conversing with Lord Graham, she found she preferred the rough, uncouth knight to the handsome, proper lord. When had that happened?

They retrieved their horses, and Guy sent the small band of guards ahead to scout the path. He and Marian followed, guided by a lantern swinging from a pole he held aloft.

The silence settled around them, punctuated by the songs of nightbirds and the sounds of night creatures roaming the forest. She swayed with the rhythm of the horse beneath her, grateful for a reprieve in conversation. The remainder of the trip gave her the solace she required to collect her thoughts.

By the time they reached the gate to her father's keep, curiosity had grown into fully formed questions in her mind. When they were safe inside the inner bailey, they dismounted, and Marian shooed away the stable boy coming to take her horse's reins.

"I will tend him. Go find your rest." She smiled as he bowed and scampered off into the night.

Marian watched Guy pull the saddle from his horse as she did the same. The rest of their party had already disappeared, leaving them alone in the stables. She groomed her gelding with a soft brush.

Guy's foreboding presence cast a shadow over them, even in the darkness of the late hour.

She returned her gelding to his stall with a gentle pat. Guy walked the length of the stable to return his stallion to his stall at the back. Marian followed, leaning against the opening as he released his hold on the beast.

"What do you call him?" she asked, breaking the tense silence. The beast lifted his head from his bucket of oats, staring at her as he chewed.

Guy rubbed the horse's thick neck beneath the copious mane. "Nix."

"A strange name for such a handsome beast." She smiled. "So similar a nature to your own."

He heaved a sigh and turned to leave the stall, nudging her out of the way.

"Have the events of the evening left you speechless, as well as cross and ill-mannered?"

He scoffed, latching the gate. When he turned, she gasped at a glow deep in his green eyes. "After listening to you and the lord of the manor dance and flirt like smitten children, 'tis a wonder I have any restraint remaining."

"Would you rather I curse and insult my host?" She blocked his path.

"You cannot seriously consider him to be an adequate

suitor?" Guy towered over her, and she shivered at the thought of him driving a fist into Graham's face. He would do it, she realized.

"Are you jealous?" The question slipped free, unbidden, and truth revealed itself in a small flicker of movement in his jaw. "You are."

The knowledge emboldened her. She ran her hand over his doublet, feeling his strength beneath the fabric. Memories of the night before flashed through her mind. His bare skin. His wicked mouth. The earthshattering pleasure he brought her.

She craved more of him.

"Admit it." Marian closed the gap between them, pushing her breasts against the solid wall of his body. "You would have killed him if he had touched me."

"I should have." He growled, his hands coming to a rest on her hips. "We have a bargain, Marian. You belong to me."

"You will ruin me? Leave me destitute and tarnished?" Her heart pounded as she drew herself close to his lips.

"I will fulfill my bargain, as will you."

"And after?"

"We will be fortunate to survive what is coming."

She paused, only a breath from his lips, drowning in his darkening gaze. "What do you mean?"

"Your sainted Lord de Bough is keeping secrets, Marian." His grip tightened.

"What did you hear?" Gooseflesh prickled along her arms.

"I heard nothing but simpering confessions of love for you," he snarled. "But my men heard enough to put de Bough in a position where I would not believe a single word that comes from his pretty mouth."

"Tell me," she begged, tugging on his tunic.

"Tomorrow eve, they are meeting to discuss their plans."

"Do you know where?"

"Aye, a small tavern just across the border. The Ram's Horn."

"I will go with you."

"Marian, they will recognize us." His scowl softened.

"Besides, your father would kill me for putting you in harm's way."

"Perhaps I should tell him of our bargain?"

He swore, a long colorful streak that warmed her heart. "Fine, but you will obey me. Do you understand?"

Pleased with the negotiation, she grinned and nodded.

He hooked his arm around her waist and pulled her into his arms. His lips covered hers. Warmth suffused her.

She wrapped her arms around his neck and deepened the kiss, craving more of what she had experienced the night before.

She groaned with disappointment when he drew away and set her down, firmly at arm's length.

"Make no mistake, Marian. I *will* claim you when the time is right. You belong to me, no other. Is that understood?"

"My body may be yours by the bonds of our agreement, but you will have to kill me to steal my heart or imprison my soul." She growled. "I belong to no man."

A wicked grin twisted his delicious lips. "Go."

She hesitated, almost in protest of his command, but she thought better of it, knowing her battles would be more difficult in the coming days. Rest would better prepare her for what was to come.

When she reached her chamber, all memory of Graham's advances had vanished, replaced by thoughts of a steely seductive determination from the handsome and terrifying Grim Knight.

Chapter Fourteen

Yet again, Guy cursed while watching dawn rise from the window of his chamber.

A new kind of restlessness—not the steady, familiar hum of unbridled rage simmering before a battle—pulsed through him. Perhaps he had been rash, showing an honest piece of his soul to Marian. Until he was certain of her regard for him, he could not reveal the extent of his past or the darkness within him.

He could not keep it from her much longer, though. Not if he intended to claim her as his. She would never forgive him. It was his olive branch, vague and useless as it was. It kept him tethered to the remaining sliver of his soul.

He dressed, determined to burn the disquiet from his mind and the agitation from his body. Had he taken her to bed as he desired, perhaps his discontent would have been alleviated. But it was not yet the right time.

She had to come willingly. Her surrender would be her choice, of her volition. He would not force her. His gentle nudges, however, would continue. Guy was not typically given to sweet words or cloying promises of passion. He took what he wanted. Marian expected him to do so, which made the challenge that much sweeter. And that much more infuriating.

Guy buttoned his doublet and pulled on his boots. Perhaps a few bouts in the lists would soothe the raging beast within him. God forgive him, but his men would suffer his foul mood, even though they had done nothing to contribute to it.

Seeing Marian with the stuffy, self-important Lord de Bough had given him an unquenchable thirst for blood. Nothing short of driving his blade through the man's gullet would suffice. For hours, Guy had suffered the agonizing pain of endless flirtation and false praise falling from the man's cursed lips.

He had not the heart to tell Marian of his true suspicions.

Not yet. Not until he uncovered irrefutable proof.

Guy recognized the glint of lust in Lord de Bough's eyes when Marian dropped her gaze, her cheeks flushed. Through the time in his company, Guy not only distrusted him more and more, but he saw the carefully crafted game the baron played in plying for Marian's hand in marriage. Such an alliance would not only strengthen his holdings but would establish him as the largest landowner on the border. If he were behind this plot with the reivers, it not only revealed his deception, it established treason.

Every word that poured from the honeyed lips of that vile snake left Guy with burning hatred. If he told Marian of his suspicion, she would claim he was jealous and defend the golden-haired serpent.

There was naught Guy could do but wait for the bastard to reveal his true nature.

Jealous. He scoffed as he abandoned his chamber, hazarding a glance at Marian's door before retreating to the lists where his men were training. Jealousy was weakness. Fury pulsed through him.

She accepted this bargain, offered herself in exchange for his service. He had never asked for her heart. Never expected it. Such a treasure could never be purchased or swindled. It must be freely given after he'd proven he deserved it.

But having her ear, her companionship, her alliance…those were tools with which he could build a foundation to move forward. 'Twas the only reason he had not yet bedded her. Let her believe him a villain, buying her innocence in exchange for his aid. He would serve her regardless, but the temptation to stoke her flames grew too delightful to ignore. He relished the passion burning within her, longed to draw it out, turning her ire and spite toward him with her words and her weapons. He would earn her contempt *and* her love.

She might not belong wholly his yet…but she would be. Body and soul.

So long as that bastard kept his hands to himself.

It had taken the duration of their return to her father's keep for him to purge the heated thoughts from his mind. Restraint came hard to him, and it tested the limits of his patience. Marian was under his care, his protection, bargain or not.

The sun shone brightly, breaking through the trees as it rose over the horizon. Captain William stood tall as he approached the men training in the lists.

"Have you anything to report, Captain?" Guy came beside him and gripped the wooden rail.

"Nothing, sir." The captain gave a brief accounting of his men and the events of the evening.

Guy's gaze rested on the men fighting in the ring. The clang of striking swords echoed through the bailey. Some of the men stopped to watched the two sparring. He cringed as their steps faltered, opening them for attack.

"You." The fight came to a halt and both combatants turned to him. Guy gestured to the taller soldier. "Stay." He pointed to the other man. "Out."

A hush fell over the gathering crowd as he stepped into the ring and removed his doublet, leaving his shirt loose. He drew his sword and circled his opponent.

The noise faded as Guy faced the soldier. The man's hair shone with threads of gold in the sunlight. Then his face faded as Guy mentally replaced it with the smirking visage of Lord de Bough.

With a shout, Guy attacked.

Sweat dampened his skin. Lifeblood poured though him as he unleashed his fury. The soldier held his own, but Guy pushed, harder and harder. Challenging, outwitting, tormenting his opponent. Gasps rippled through the crowd as he lunged for a final blow, pinning the man to the dirt, his blade pressed to the soldier's throat.

"Sir Guy!" The shout echoed through the crowd as though traveling through a long stone corridor.

The face of the pompous lord disappeared, once more revealing the gritted, bloody expression of the nameless soldier beneath him. He shoved back, pushing himself to his feet.

Ignoring the horrified faces of those who had gathered

around the ring, he ducked beneath the railing and strode to the water bucket. Guy poured the first ladleful over his head, letting the cool water sluice down his face.

"What was the meaning of that?" Her irate voice filled the air around him.

He dipped another ladleful and drank it.

"Do you treat all of your men in such a brutal manner?"

When he finally turned, he observed the way her eyes widened when she saw his drenched form. She blinked, watching water drip from his face to his chest, matting the fabric to his skin. The heat in her gaze turned icy again as she refocused her ire.

"What I do with my men is none of your concern."

"You are here by order of the king. These are *his* men, not yours. They are *my* guests and will be treated with dignity. I will not have you beating any one of them to a bloody pulp because you cannot control your temper."

"You cannot train as a soldier, as a knight, and not spill blood, vixen."

"*That* was not training. You would have killed him had I not intervened." She stood taller, glaring at him. "Whatever internal battle you wage, I will not have you unleash it upon these soldiers. Turn it against the reivers to sate your bloodlust."

"My methods are not up for negotiation."

"They are as long as you are a guest in my home."

"Perhaps I shall speak to your father and ask his opinion of my methods?"

Her face blanched, bringing a feral grin to his lips.

"I can explain *everything* to him." The threat hung in the air between them.

"Bastard," she hissed beneath her breath. "Curse you to the depths of hell."

He chuckled and left her standing there, defeated. After retrieving his doublet, he returned to her side. "Come, vixen."

"Do not order me about like some trained bitch." Marian smoothed her skirts, refusing to budge.

"Ride with me." He coaxed with a soft voice, coming closer

to her.

Her icy demeanor melted enough for him to see the warm, welcoming woman beneath it. He caught his breath at her beauty, holding it as he admired her heart. *She is a good woman, too good for the likes of me.*

"Fine." Her response pulled him from the thoughts stirring his mind. She strode toward the stables.

He followed, growling at pages and stable hands along the way. She eyed him with annoyance when he snapped at a lad leading his stallion. He suppressed the urge to growl at everyone and instead set to saddling his horse.

When they had escaped the confines of the keep and entered the gentle shaded canopy of the forest, the horses fell into step alongside each other. Guy's shoulders relaxed as Nix absorbed his agitation, and he gently stroked the beast's neck to soothe him.

"Perhaps you need someone to stroke your neck and feed you treats to calm your temper?" Marian's observation broke the silence between them.

"Are you offering your services?" he asked, flashing a teasing grin.

"I have already made a devil's bargain with you." She narrowed her eyes at him. "What more could you possibly want from me?"

"Everything, Marian," he crooned as the tension ebbed and flowed between them, like a tide, gradually drawing them together.

She sighed. "Where are you leading me?"

"To the tavern where the meeting is to be held this eve." He turned his attention to the stretch of road before him. "I want to get an idea of what to expect. The last thing I wish to do is walk into a trap."

"Why bring me?"

"You know this place, these lands. These people. I require your opinion to form a successful plan."

"I do know them." She regarded him carefully. "Why ask for my aid on this matter when any of my guards would suffice?"

"Can I not enjoy the pleasure of your company?" At her scowl, he laughed. "Truth be told, you are the only one I trust."

"How endearing."

"We struck an accord, Marian." He sobered, watching her steadily. "I intend to keep my end of the bargain, but not because I am an honorable man who wishes to protect these people and your father's lands. My motivations are purely selfish." He smirked, allowing the implication of his words to fill the void.

She shifted in her saddle, not meeting his gaze. When she did, he saw a fire of need in the depths of her eyes.

"If we are to uncover this plot, we must work together to roust the villain behind it." He took a deep breath. "We must have men inside the tavern and out. We must have eyes everywhere."

Marian shook her head and snorted. "You cannot send soldiers in. They stand out…like a gilded carriage in a mud hole."

"What do you propose?"

A grin split her lips as a plan formed in her mind. "I shall send a message to my little band of men. They are known in this area and spend time on each side of the border. They can be our eyes and ears."

He scoffed. "You intend to send your ragged band of outlaws?"

"Aye." Her eyes gleamed like gemstones in the morning light. "My men do as I bid, and I do not require threats or beatings to ensure compliance."

He rolled his eyes. Did she truly think so little of him? His reputation had persisted for years, and he had never wished to correct the assumptions surrounding his name, his grim title. Until he met her.

"And what of their allegiance?" Guy asked. "Will they stay true to you or sell their services and honor to whomever offers the most gold?"

"They are my friends. My family." Marian's voice softened. "I have known them since I was a child. They found me wandering the forests when I was five."

"Why were you alone in the forest?"

Marian fixed her attention on the road. "When my mother died, I was devastated. My father, overwhelmed by his own grief, locked himself away. He knew not what to do with his young daughter.

"One day, my nursemaid took me to pick berries in the forest, thinking it would distract me from the somber atmosphere at the keep. I wandered off, chasing butterflies through a meadow. The farther I went, the darker the woods became. I was lost."

Guy listened silently, not wanting to break the spell of her tale. 'Twas the first time she had revealed anything of her past, of her heart. He studied her proud, graceful profile. Even in such a vulnerable moment, she glowed with confidence.

"When darkness fell, I found a small hut with smoke billowing from the chimney. I knocked, unsure of what I would find, but I was hungry and tired." She smiled. "Four men stood inside the cottage. They took pity on me, gave me food and a small bed on which to sleep. In the morning, they returned me to the edge of the forest near the keep and told me I was safe. Home."

A soft smile curved her lips. "Over the years, they turned away from thieving and became my scouts. My informants. My friends."

"Did you tell your father?"

"He knows the kindness of strangers brought me home." Marian laughed. "But he does not know their names or their exploits."

"Or that they are your band of merry outlaws?"

Marian gently shook her head. "I do not wish to cause him more concern than necessary. With his health, he…" She let the words drift off, as though the implications were obvious.

"And you think they will agree to this plan?" Guy asked. "Your merry men."

"Aye. There are none in the world so loyal." Her smile infected him with its assurance. "Would you like to meet them?"

His brows rose in surprise. "You wish to grant me a personal introduction?"

"So long as you do not threaten or cross blades with them." She twisted in the saddle to study him. "I cannot vouch for their actions should they take a disliking to you."

"Are you concerned for my safety, vixen?"

"I am more concerned about how I would explain your horrid death and my miraculous escape unscathed."

Guy's laugh echoed through the trees. It had been too long since he had freely laughed. It felt good. Liberating.

Her jaw dropped, her tongue lolling at the sound. She snapped her mouth closed and blinked twice.

"What?" he asked.

"I have never heard you laugh."

"Most have not. Count yourself among a very few." He shifted uncomfortably. "Perhaps the only."

"Surely, that cannot be true?" Her smile warmed the cold recesses of his heart.

"Perhaps." He shrugged. "Make no mention of it. I would hate to ruin my reputation."

"'Twould be horrid to reveal that the wicked, brooding Grim Knight has a delightful laugh."

Guy grimaced at the thought. No one knew of the horrors he had endured, had captured and molded around himself like armor. He could honestly not remember the last time he'd permitted himself a joyful laugh. He had never allowed another person to glimpse the darkest, rawest part of his soul…and yet, he longed to reveal it to her. To let her choose whether to embrace him, all of him, or to shun him completely.

"After the horrors I have seen, the atrocities I have committed, 'tis a wonder I remember how to laugh."

Marian regarded him steadily, her smile fading. "Is that why they call you the Grim Knight?"

"Nay." He inhaled deeply, settling the riot inside him before speaking. "The grim refers not to my demeanor so much as my penchant for inflicting cruel death."

"Surely, the rumors exaggerate?" She met his gaze and held it, unflinching. "Making you into a formidable legend by which to bring order from chaos."

"I have told you before, Marian, I am not a good man." He turned away, unable to bear the hope in her eyes. Fearing its dissolution if he revealed the truth.

"Tell me why you believe yourself to be beyond salvation."

Her soft words drifted over him like a soothing balm, but tension knotted in the pit of his stomach.

"God's blood." He swallowed hard and sighed in defeat. "As a young knight, I was sent with a small band of men to quell an uprising on an island in the English channel. The French had taken control of it, and it came to the king's attention they were using it as a base to smuggle spies into England, to instigate displeasure with the monarchy among the populace."

She listened quietly, attentively as they rode through the woods toward the border.

"When we arrived, we ransacked every village. Overturned every stone. The villagers knew nothing and swore their fealty to England." He tightened his grip on the reins. "Until one night, a band of men attacked us in the dead of night, leaving half the battalion dead or wounded.

"We attempted to retreat but were met with resistance from the villagers. The same people who had sworn loyalty to the crown."

"What did you do?" Marian asked, her voice trembling.

"The captain at arms commanded we defend ourselves, and the situation quickly escalated. The soldiers began burning homes. Entire villages turned to infernos against the blue skies." He blinked, trying to banish the haunting memory of protests and wails of grief forever lodged in his mind. "The survivors took refuge in a church near the sea.

"We locked the doors and burned it to the ground." The dying screams still haunted his waking moments as well as his nightmares.

"Oh, merciful God." Marian clapped a hand over her mouth, her face pale, her hands shaking.

"Since that day, I swore I would do what needed to be done, regardless of cost. When word reached the king of my involvement and our success in quelling the treason…" He stiffened. "I was rewarded with a title and lands for my service to the crown. Whispers of the horrors of that venture left my reputation tarnished. The Grim Knight had risen victorious from the ashes. But their blood stains my hands…and my conscience."

Guy finally turned to her, his lips set in a thin line as he awaited her censure. Tears streaked her lovely cheeks, and sorrow swam in her hazel eyes.

"Do you believe me now, Marian, when I say I am not a good man?" A heavy ache settled around his heart.

"I know not what to believe." She wiped her tears away. "But I know there is always hope of salvation…even for the most tarnished soul."

He scoffed, dropping his gaze to his gloved hands. Even now, he could see where the blood had been. Silence drifted between them as they crossed a small creek. The sound of flowing water and birdsong filled the void but did nothing to dispel the anguish in his chest.

Revealing his past had been a risky calculation on his part. Even now, he felt distance growing between them. He cursed himself, but deep inside, he knew the truth—there could be nothing between them without this revelation.

And the relief he hoped to feel was nowhere to be found.

"The tavern is just ahead." Marian pointed to a bend in the road.

Guy allowed the conversation to drift back to their plans, away from the small glimpse he had allowed into his shielded heart. If there was a merciful God, he prayed he had not burned all hope of earning Marian's favor.

For a man such as him deserved neither salvation nor a woman so pure of heart.

Chapter Fifteen

After visiting the tavern, Guy fell silent. Marian embraced the peace between them, but she wondered if his sudden pensiveness was due to his painful revelation. Even she had not been prepared for the cruel and violent tale. His actions haunted him, both in name and in bearing. She wanted to hate him for the brutality, but beneath his brusque words, she heard his regret, the toll it had taken upon his soul.

Instead of pushing it aside and casting judgment, she listened. Part of her pondered what her own actions would have been if confronted with such a choice. Her heart ached, both for the innocents he'd slaughtered and for his tormented soul.

Guy trusted her. Even with such confidence in *her*, he had told her not to trust him. But she *did* trust him, even though it went against her better judgment.

Whatever was building between them, she could not quite make sense of it. At first, their tentative truce had been borne of their reckless bargain. But as the days passed, there seemed to be *something* tugging at them, an undercurrent in their interactions. Surely, they were not friends, nor were they lovers. Partners of a sort…but more than that if his words were to be believed.

And now he had unveiled his past to her. A past he kept closer than a secret.

Pushing aside her internal struggle, she led the way through the forest. If they were to succeed in their quest, they needed to focus and obtain help. Part of her wondered at the wisdom of leading him to the lair of her trusted men. She had not seen them since the night Guy encountered her in the forest, concealed in her black hood.

They knew of the encounter, of the dangers surrounding their excursions. She had sent messages through her servants. Her system of conveying messages back and forth had worked seamlessly for years. With Guy's watchful eye on her, she had sent only the most important information. What would they say when she arrived with this man she claimed to abhor?

Marian prayed she was not wrong to bring her men into this volatile situation. Deep in her heart, she knew it was the only way to infiltrate the tavern without arousing suspicion. One of them would hear something. All it took was one small kernel of proof, and the whole plot would unravel. Determined, she forged ahead, bracing herself for the oncoming conflict.

The small cottage appeared in the distance, nestled deep within the forest canopy, almost hidden from view. She smiled at the surfacing memories. As an only child, she had longed for a brother or sister, someone in whom she could confide. A fellow mischief-maker.

Over the years, these men had become her brothers of a sort. Willing to fight beside her, willing to die for her. They trusted her judgment, and in turn, she placed her faith in theirs.

"Leave the horses here." She dismounted and tied her gelding to a nearby tree.

Guy followed suit, not saying anything as he came alongside her, eyeing the cottage with suspicion.

"Do try not to insult them." Marian smiled at the way he tensed midstep. "Oh, and do not make any sudden movements."

His only response was a low growl. The sound reverberated through her like a bell. She cleared her throat and took the lead.

After two taps on the solid wood, a small slat in the door opened and an eye appeared.

"Butcher," she murmured.

"Marian." A surprised disembodied voice echoed through the gap. It slammed closed, and the door opened.

Samuel paused when he caught sight of the knight behind her, and he blocked the door with his broad body. "What is he doing here?"

"If you allow me inside, I will explain." Marian kept her tone soothing and calm.

Inside the cottage, she relaxed at the sight of the familiar faces. John, Michael, and Jack sat at the small table. Samuel closed the door behind them.

All four men drew their blades.

"Marian, by the saints, why have you brought *him* here?" Jack scowled at Guy.

"Lower your weapons." She waved her hand, her heart thundering in her chest, fear threatening to choke her. Had she miscalculated? Would they kill him? She shoved aside her uncertainty and plowed forward. "I require your help."

"You working with him?" Samuel jabbed his hilt in Guy's direction.

"I am."

"You trust him?" John asked, slightly lowering his weapon.

"I do."

Marian met Guy's gaze. His expression looked carved from stone, solid and unyielding. She saw a glimmer of amusement in his eyes, as though he wanted these men to fight. She could not, would not allow them to shed blood here. There were bigger threats to face outside these walls.

Begrudgingly, her men sheathed their blades. Muttered curses floated around her, but the tension had abated with her simple declaration.

"We believe someone is ordering the reiver attacks." Marian straightened at their stunned expressions.

"What do you mean?" Samuel took a seat near the fire.

"*Every* attack for the last year has been on my father's land. None of the other lords have had an issue with reivers." Her eyes narrowed. "Neither of them has offered their support without very specific conditions. At first, I believed it was because of cowardice, but now I see they have nothing to gain by coming to our aid."

"What of Lord de Bough?" Michael, the youngest, asked. "He has shown his support."

"Aye, I thought much the same. Until I realized his support also came with strings." Marian inclined her head. "He asked me to wed him. Repeatedly. He has made his intentions quite clear. Until I am his wife, he will not extend resources or men to stop the violence on our land."

"Bastard." Jack swore and the others shook their heads, muttering under their breath. "Why come to us for help? Since his lot appeared"—he gestured toward Guy—"we are confined here, unable to do much but sit on our arses and sharpen our blades."

"I understand your frustration." Marian noted the way he blamed Guy for their position, and while she didn't entirely disagree with him, the knight's presence had proven more of a blessing than any of them realized. "But there are things his men cannot do."

John scoffed. "Such as?"

"There is a meeting tonight at the Ram's Horn," Guy said, his voice low and even. "We need you to investigate."

"What? You want us to be your spies?" John and the others shared a glance.

"Aye. We need you to blend into the crowd, search out information that may help us."

"Who are we spying on?" Jack asked.

"Lord de Bough." Marian struggled to keep her emotions in check. "We overheard something about this meeting tonight at the tavern. I want to know for certain whether he is behind this plot with the reivers."

"And if he is not?" Samuel leaned forward, resting his elbows on his knees.

"Whatever he is doing, I want to know." She gritted her teeth. "There is something afoot, and I cannot rest until I know of his plans."

"Aye, we can do that." John stood, arching his back. He smiled, his face the familiar comfort of her childhood, and she warmed through. 'Twas he who opened the cottage door when she was a wee lass seeking refuge and shelter. He had been a handsome lad of six and ten then. Now he led the four of them, all around the same age, under her direction.

"Thank you, John." She nearly burst with relief. "Thank you, all."

At their somber nods, she turned to Guy. "Give them the details of your plan."

Guy stepped forward and explained what his men had overheard, then he laid out the details of the evening's events as he thought they would proceed. To their credit, none of her men protested. They even nodded in agreement to much of the plan, only interjecting to correct minor details or to apply a new strategy when they met a stone wall.

Seeing Guy with her men imbued her with a sense of pride. Desire unfurled within her as he spoke. She bit her lower lip to keep from interrupting—he had things well in hand. Instead, she focused on his words, trying to ignore the pull of his presence by her side.

"Marian and I will wait at the edge of the forest," Guy finished. "If there is trouble, we will be ready to come to your aid."

Her cheeks warmed as her men looked between them. "This must be done quietly. I do not want Lord de Bough to know we suspect him."

The four men nodded in agreement.

"We shall rendezvous here if all goes to plan." She swallowed the lump in her throat. "Should they suspect you, head to the keep. The guards will allow you inside if you tell them you come with a message for me."

"It shall be done," Jack said, a smile on his lips.

"No bloodshed if it can be helped." Marian's pointed stare lingered on each man in turn to emphasize the importance of her instruction. She stopped at Guy. "Especially you."

He lifted his hands in supplication. "I would never disobey you, my lady."

The four men snickered at his comment, but quickly covered their amusement with their hands when she frowned. They spent some time going over the plan a second time before abandoning the cottage and heading to the tavern.

The sun drifted low on the horizon, casting long shadows across the fields. Her men veered toward the tavern, singing and jesting as they swayed in their saddles.

She and Guy tethered their horses deep in the trees and crept to the hedgerow where they could remain concealed as they waited. She sat in the dirt, leaning against a tree. Guy joined her, their shoulders brushing.

Nightingale song drifted around them along with the distant chatter of tavern patrons staggering toward the village, but otherwise, silence filled the evening air.

"Your men are loyal to you."

Guy's observation surprised her. Pride and pleasure blossomed in her chest.

"They are."

"You are fortunate."

"Are your men not loyal to you?" she asked, turning to study him.

"None are loyal to me. Only to the crown." He kept his focus on the tavern as he spoke, not meeting her gaze.

"Perhaps your byname instills more fear than loyalty?"

Guy shrugged. "I did not choose it."

"But you chose to embrace the identity, did you not?"

His green eyes shifted, locking with hers. They sparkled in the fading light. "My life…this life…is not of my choosing. If I could do it again, I would choose differently."

The sadness in his confession struck her. She pitied him, the emptiness he must feel. Her heart ached for the man before her, for the sad, lonely boy he must have been. For the calloused man he was forced to become.

Instead of dwelling on the past, she offered a kind smile.

"If you could have anything in the world, what would you choose?"

She nudged him when he did not respond.

He cocked his head, his gaze softening. "You."

Marian's heart ceased beating for a moment. She licked her lips, trying to form a response in her mind. Nothing came.

He had rendered her speechless with his blunt honesty.

"I—"

The sound of galloping horses thundered past their hiding spot. They fell back into silence as the small group approached the tavern. As the men dismounted, she studied their profiles. None seemed familiar. When she turned to ask Guy if he recognized the men, she froze.

He slid forward, studying the men, his jaw set. "De Bough's men," he said simply.

"Are you certain?"

"Absolutely."

When the group entered the tavern, Guy and Marian each held their breath and waited.

Gone was the easy conversation from earlier. Knowing the men they sought were inside the tavern—as they had planned— left her restless with anticipation. But time drew on and on into darkness. She leaned against the tree and closed her eyes.

Marian started when Guy nudged her. Had she fallen asleep? What had happened? She straightened, her ears pricking at the sound of arguing voices. The shouts grew closer. Louder.

"Quick!" Guy dragged her to her feet and took her hand as they ran into the forest.

The sound of snapping branches echoed behind them, followed by shouts. Cries of alarm. Panic coursed through her veins. She darted toward the place where they had tied the horses, fear burning in her chest making it hard to breathe.

Where were they going? It was dark. Too dark. She could not remember the way.

When the horses came into view, she barely had time to whisper a prayer of gratitude before Guy hoisted her into the saddle and slapped the gelding's hindquarter.

Marian gathered the reins in her hands and drove her heels into the horse's flanks. Blindly, they raced through the forest, heading for a place of refuge.

She glanced over her shoulder. Guy's black stallion was following close behind with him astride. Marian exhaled with relief and leaned low over her horse's neck.

Whatever happened at the tavern, they had been found.

A chill ran down her spine as a lump of regret formed in her throat. *What* happened in the tavern? What happened to her men?

She prayed hard. *Please let them live.*

Chapter Sixteen

The sounds of their pursuers—crashing branches, hooves pounding dirt—faded into the distance as Guy pushed his stallion harder and harder. With every breath, the sounds grew more muffled, lost to the darkening forest.

His gaze remained firmly fixed on Marian and her gelding ahead of him, weaving deftly around trees, seeking the path to the cottage where they had met with her men earlier.

Something had gone terribly wrong. It had been wise to remain out of the tavern, as they would have been recognized by all within the establishment. The men she had sent in blended into the wood, making them the perfect spies.

But the fact that they were currently running for their lives indicated they had misjudged something, their intentions had been uncovered. How they managed to ascertain his and Marian's location in the forest left him both infuriated and puzzled. It was all he could do to refrain from turning around to face their pursuers with his blade drawn.

Never in his life had he run from a fight. Distaste and shame burned in his gut at the thought of appearing a coward and fleeing into the forest like a terrified stag. But it was imperative they keep their identities hidden…unless those too had been exposed within the tavern. *God's blood, teeth, and bones.*

Ahead, Marian slowed her horse to a walk, and Guy eased his own mount to match her pace. She seemed to nudge the gelding down the path only on instinct. The light had disappeared completely, casting the trees and brush into darkness and shadows.

A flurry of possibilities assailed him as they wove through the dense forest. He fully intended to uncover the truth, but not until Marian was safely out of harm's way.

When the small cottage came into view, lit by strands of

moonlight from behind the clouds, he drew in a deep breath of relief. They had made it.

Marian dismounted and led her horse to a small open-sided stable at the back of the cottage. She tied the reins and stroked her horse's neck, whispering to him in a voice sweeter than honey.

What he would not give to hear her use such a tone with him. Guy tensed at the fleeting thought, then shook his head. He climbed down from his saddle and tied the stallion beside her horse. The beasts' heavy breaths echoed through the small enclosure, mirroring his own.

Once he had ensured the horses were secure, he turned to find her watching him. Before he could speak, she retreated to the cottage. His heart still raced from their narrow escape, blood pounding in his ears, his muscles tense as though bracing for a fight. He took two deep breaths, inhaling then exhaling. It echoed in the narrow space like a low growl, making the horses turn, ears flicking with uncertainty.

Inside, he found Marian adding wood to the fire, stoking embers to life. Light flickered and shadows danced on the walls as she moved before the flames. With a final glance into the silence of the night, he pulled the door closed, securing it firmly behind him. He was reaching for the latch to lock it when she spoke.

"Best not lock it."

Guy spun to face her. "You would leave us exposed?"

"My men are still out there. They will return."

"When they do, they can knock, just as we did." He dropped the latch into place and secured the door with a board braced across it.

Her eyes narrowed, but she did not argue. Instead, Marian collapsed into a chair beside the fire and rested her head against the wall.

"How did they know where we were hiding?" Her soft question mingled with the sound of crackling logs.

"'Tis possible they did not know exactly where or who we were, but they knew *someone* was watching the tavern." Guy crossed to the hearth and leaned against the wall, fixing his gaze on her.

"Do you believe it was a trap?"

"Possibly. However, I fear your men found themselves in the midst of traitors and could not escape without being detected."

Her mouth parted with a silent gasp. "I am a fool for sending them into harm's way."

"They would follow you to hell itself if you asked it of them." *As would I,* he added silently. His heart ached at the agony etched in her face. "Do not fret, Marian. Your band of thieves can surely take on whatever threat they encounter."

His words were an attempt to ease her conscience, to soothe the worry creasing her delicate brow and stealing her spirit. But he was no poet, and words so often failed him. Action, however, left little doubt of his intentions. So he sat with her, surrounded by unanswered questions and silent concern for her men.

"I cannot sit here doing nothing." Marian rose and smoothed her torn skirts, ripped by gnarled branches and briars as they raced through the forest in their escape. "I must go to them."

Guy blocked the door. "I cannot allow you to leave."

"You are not my keeper." Her steely gaze held his.

"No." He stood his ground. "You will not leave this cottage."

"I command you to step aside." She gritted her teeth.

"We have a bargain, Marian."

Fire flickered in her eyes. "What does that have to do with this?"

"Everything." Guy crowded her, bringing himself close enough to feel her heat, to hear a catch in her breath. "When we struck that bargain, I vowed not only to aid you in stopping the reivers, but to protect you from harm."

"I remember no such agreement."

"When you promised your body as payment, you bound yourself to me." He leaned close, inhaling her intoxicating scent, his lips a breath from brushing her cheek. "I will die protecting what belongs to me."

"I belong to no man." Her tone wavered, but she made no attempt to escape his proximity.

A soft chuckle escaped him. She could fight it with every breath, but her body had already surrendered to the tension pulling them together. Marian glared at him, radiating passion and independence. A woman of wit and beauty with a warrior's spirit. Her denial only further enflamed his desire.

"When I had you in my bed with my mouth on your sweet cunt, you sang a different song, vixen." He trailed his nose across her cheek, savoring the way her body trembled and swayed closer.

"You delight in tormenting me." The words were meant to bite, but her voice softened with each one uttered.

"I delight in *you*, Marian." His hand settled at the curve of her hip as he sought her lips with his own.

The kiss dredged desire from the blackness of memory, pulling it into the light. He cradled her jaw in his hand, delving his tongue between her lips. Her mewling response ignited the embers she'd left burning inside his cold heart.

This woman feared nothing. She lived and bled for those she loved, willing to sacrifice all for peace and prosperity. He wished he could be the kind of man she deserved, an honorable man. But he was not. A gaping hole burned where his soul had once been, stolen against his will. Kissing her, loving Marian gave him hope. He prayed she would see beneath the stone encasing his heart.

Marian flung her arms around his neck, pulling herself flush against his firm body, her nimble fingers threading through his hair. She teased his scalp with her fingertips and tugged the strands in fistfuls. Her mouth opened, slanting over his, inviting him to plunder all she possessed.

Hers was not a surrender so much as a siege. Any seduction he had planned fled his mind when she rubbed against his thigh. Her soft moans echoed in his ear as he kissed a path along her jaw and down her neck.

"I may expire for want of you," Guy murmured against her

skin as he gathered her skirts into his fists, bunching them around her waist. His fingertips brushed the apex of her sex. She was slick, ready for him. "Wicked vixen. Your words say one thing, but your body knows the truth."

"What truth?" She arched her hips into his hand, grinding herself into his palm.

"You. Are. Mine." He slid two fingers deep into her, wishing it were his cock.

"Guy." She gasped, biting her lip as he thrusted and withdrew, again and again.

He ignored the press of his cock against her hip. Not here. Not now. Guy would not take her against the wall of a cottage. He would savor her, feast on her for hours before burying himself inside her to stake his claim. In time…she would be his in time. For now, he would bring her sweet release, bind her to him with pleasure.

The scent of her arousal drove him mad. He longed to taste her, but there would be more time later. He quickened his pace, adding pressure to the apex, her body humming beneath his touch. She rocked her hips against his hand. With an arm banded around her, he held her tight and increased the pressure.

She writhed against him, climbing toward the inevitable precipice. He pressed soft kisses to her throat, dragging his lips along her tender skin and nipping softly with his teeth. With a sharp inhale, her climax seized her, pulling her tight as a bowstring.

Panting, she slowly relaxed against him. Her body gently relinquished his hold, and her shredded skirts fell into place, hiding the evidence of her release.

Guy kissed her jaw. "God's blood, you are a sight to behold when you find your pleasure."

She turned, and her lips brushed his in a tender kiss. Her hand slid over his cock, still hard and thick beneath his hose.

"What of you?" Marian gripped him through the fabric.

Her bold touch cracked the steel of his resolve.

Guy hissed in a breath and covered her hand with his. "Not this eve, vixen."

"Do you not enjoy my touch?"

"I crave it more than my next breath." He took a moment to steady his rampaging thoughts. "But we need to return to the keep."

Marian drew back, releasing him. His sigh of relief ended in a growl of frustration.

"My men have not returned."

"They have not." Guy ran a hand over his face.

"We should search for them."

"*You* will return to the keep." He grasped her shoulders and held her fast. "I cannot guarantee your safety here."

"I never asked for you to protect me." She scowled.

Thud. Crack.

They jumped away from the door.

The startling noise was followed by a soft knock echoing through the wood in an odd rhythm. Marian gasped and pushed him aside before unlatching the lock and throwing away the barrier.

As Marian opened the door, Guy pulled his dagger from the sheath on his hip and braced for whoever was on the other side.

A figure stumbled inside. "My lady." Relief filled the man's voice at the sight of Marian.

"Michael." She rushed to his side and offered support as he stumbled into the room.

Guy quickly surveyed the outside and closed the door. "Where are the others?" he asked, turning to the lone man.

Breathless, Michael dropped into a chair by the hearth. Dirt and blood, illuminated by flickering firelight, streaked his face.

"They fled. I know not where." He winced as Marian assessed his injuries. "Samuel is dead."

Marian paused her ministrations. "How?" she asked, her mouth set in a grim line.

"One of Lord de Bough's men." He held her gaze. "They must have suspected our purpose. Turned on us. Jack shouted to warn you, and half the men fled. Forgive me."

Guy nearly grabbed the man by the throat and hoisted him from the chair. Her men had betrayed their location. He stepped closer, fury thundering through his veins.

"You put her in danger," he growled, his voice low and menacing. "I should kill all of you."

Marian spun to glare at him before turning back to the injured man. "'Tis of no concern now. Do you require a healer?"

The man shook his head. "'Tis but a few scratches and bruises. I shall be fine with rest."

With a nod, Marian stood and turned to face Guy. "We need to find them."

"*You* will return to the keep."

"I cannot rest until I know they are safe."

"Return to the keep." Guy clenched his hands into fists and took a steadying breath. "I will gather my soldiers, and we will form a party to search for your men."

Marian blinked in surprise. "Truly?"

"Aye." He gestured toward the door. "We must make haste."

With a nod, she strode for the door like a soldier to battle. Guy followed her, unsure of what lay ahead of them in the dark forest.

They rode in silence until the keep came into view. Marian approached the gate first, allowing the guards to see her face before it swung open at her command.

When they dismounted in the bailey, Guy caught Marian by the arm, halting her. Her luminous eyes met his.

"Whatever happens, remain here, in the safety of the keep." He licked his lips. "Promise me, Marian."

She studied his face, her eyes narrowing slightly. Finally, with a sigh, she conceded with a firm nod.

"Good. Gather your allies. We will need them."

"If you find John and Jack, please bring them here."

Guy took her hand and brushed his lips across her knuckles.

She stepped closer, gently squeezing his hand. "Return with haste." *And be safe.* He saw the unspoken words deep in her eyes as he turned to go.

After he spoke to the captain and organized a small party to search for the missing men, Guy mounted his horse and spurred him toward the gate. While they searched, he would return to the tavern to uncover the events of the evening as they had unraveled.

Someone knew something, and he would drag it from their lips by force if necessary.

With Marian ensconced behind the stone walls of the keep, safe and protected, he would unleash hell. There would be blood. And he would gladly spill it to protect the woman he loved.

Chapter Seventeen

The sun dragged across the sky with agonizing slowness. It had been hours since Guy and his soldiers rode out.

Marian attempted to busy herself. She rallied her allies, informing them of treasonous whispers and their deadly implications. Those she entrusted took her warning to heart, moving quickly to ensure the keep and the people within it were well protected and prepared for whatever might come. She bustled from room to room, telling those loyal to her of the threat.

All the while, Guy's words echoed through her mind. *You are mine.*

Try as she might, she could not shake the effect those three words had on her. The thought of a man treating her as a possession had always repulsed her, but his words struck a chord of truth within her, one she could not deny. The same possessive nature rang deep inside her when she thought of him.

Their bargain had been made in haste and under duress, and she had been altered by it. Though she did not wish to admit how much. Even in the days immediately following their agreement, she found herself more and more at ease with the arrangement. In truth, she had found herself longing for his attention, his touch, his presence. His confession of his past sins should have deterred her, but it only proved he wished to have no secrets, no barrier between them.

Even in the chaotic aftermath of their escape from the tavern, his focus had been solely on her protection. Her comfort. Her pleasure. No matter how hard she searched her heart for a reason to push him away, his actions spoke beyond words. His touch, his tender care for her needs superseded her own. Could he truly care for her?

There had been ample opportunity for Guy to lay claim to

his half of the bargain, to the complete surrender of her body to his lustful desires. Yet he had not acted upon it. Perhaps he was not the grim, cold-hearted monster the stories would have her believe.

He was brusque and callous, selfish and condescending. And yet, somewhere beneath the black garments and dark scowl lay the heart of a true knight willing to sacrifice himself for those in his care. Sir Guy Silverthorne, the Grim Knight, was truly an enigma. A man cloaked in shadow and secrets, armed with a sharp mind and a spiteful tongue.

Marian paused in the doorway of the great hall, surveying the activity in the bailey. Servants bustled around, carrying linens and baskets of vegetables. The chickens scuttled beneath their feet, and the muffled whinnies of horses echoed from the stables.

'Twas just as every other day, except things felt…different. Incomplete. Untethered. As though the sky would fall at any moment. A sense of dread settled in her gut. She pressed her hand to her bodice in an attempt to stifle the unease stirring within her.

Perhaps she should consult her father. His wisdom would soothe the concern twisting through her mind like tendrils of thorny vines. She looked over her shoulder to the empty great hall, silent as a tomb.

Earlier, Anne had told her of her father's weakened state. Serving as both servant and healer, the maid took her position quite seriously. And since her father's decline in health, Marian had relied heavily on the woman's expertise. Their bond extended beyond the reach of social station. Anne taught her all she knew of herbs and healing, and Marian embraced the knowledge with gratitude and curiosity. Combined, their care would ensure her father's comfort and longevity.

Marian frowned. She could not bother her father with such trivial matters, not until they uncovered solid evidence of their neighbors' treachery. If he knew of the dangerous situation in which she had placed herself, he would marry her off without a second thought. For her safety, of course.

Marian straightened, her spine becoming rigid at the thought. Absolutely not. With a deep breath, she cleared her mind. All she could do was wait for Guy's return and pray he located the rest of her men.

A shout at the gate drew her attention. She stepped into the bailey, hope fluttering in her chest like a bird taking flight. Had Guy returned? Had he found her men?

As the gate opened, an unfamiliar horse stepped into view. Upon its back, sat Graham.

Hope dissolved to revulsion. Icy fingers of fear trailed along her neck when his gaze lighted upon her, a wicked smile curving his lips. Once upon a time, she had counted him among her trusted friends. They had grown up together, shared time laughing and exploring.

But ever since their encounter in London and his persistent requests for her hand in marriage, she'd found his company not only tedious but uncomfortable. Her attendance at his feast had left her with a distinct distaste for his presence. Almost as if he could sense her hesitation, his eyes narrowed as he dismounted.

She forced a congenial smile and strode across the grounds.

"My lord, to what do we owe the honor of this visit?" Marian clasped her hands before her but maintained distance between them.

"I was out riding and decided to call upon you and your father." His golden smile reappeared. "I trust your father's health has improved?"

"It has," Marian lied.

"Is it possible I might speak with him?" Graham smoothed a hand over his thick, blond hair.

"My apologies, but he is asleep at the moment, resting after a morning of activity." The lies came easily, slipping from her tongue with little effort. "Perhaps you could return another day."

The sunlight shifted behind the clouds, casting them into shadow. Graham's eyes darkened—whether a trick of the light or a change in demeanor, she could not be certain.

"I see." He pressed his lips into a thin line.

"Would you care for some refreshment? Some wine,

perhaps?" Marian gestured toward the great hall, even though her skin crawled at the thought of spending any time alone with him.

"I would..." Graham's words fell silent at a rise of commotion behind them.

They turned to find the gate swinging open, and a small band of horses loped into the space, their riders sitting tall and straight...save one, who slumped over the back of a massive, black stallion.

"Guy." Marian's voice broke as she rushed to his side.

The stallion danced as Captain William tossed the reins to a stable boy. Guy's limp form was draped across his saddle, tied with rope to secure him from slipping free. His soft breaths caressed her fingers as she lifted his head. He was alive. Thank the saints.

"What happened?" Marian rounded on the captain as she reached for the ropes securing Guy.

"We were ambushed." The captain blanched. "I managed to get the men free, but Sir Guy...he raced into the thick of it." His eyes widened, and he shook his head. "All the stories I heard about the Grim Knight...I have never seen such ferocity and brute force until today."

Fear ripped through her as an image of Guy brandishing his sword as he charged into battle filled her mind.

"Help me."

Several soldiers came to her aid, pulling him from the saddle. He groaned, his eyes fluttering at the movement. Dried blood and dirt smeared his face. Trickles of fresh blood ran across his forehead and down his cheek.

"Guy, can you hear me?" Marian cradled his face in her hands. "Please."

He moaned and lifted his head. Those striking green eyes met hers. A lopsided smile formed at the sight of her. "Marian."

Relief filled her. At least he was coherent. "Take him to his chambers. Fetch Anne."

Guy's smile disappeared as his attention drifted to something behind her. "You," he growled, leveraging himself to bear his weight, standing but stumbling. "Bloody coward."

Marian turned. Graham stood several paces behind her, carefully watching the interaction. His usually bright disposition had faded to the gloom of a stormy day. He held his ground, his eyes narrowed, jaw tight.

"I will kill you." Guy's threat echoed like a sword strike through the bailey. "This is my vow." He leaned close to her and whispered, "Do not trust him, Marian. He is a traitor."

"Take him up now, please." Marian smoothed her hands on her skirts and watched them lead Guy to the great hall.

"I cannot imagine what has gotten into him." Marian turned to Graham, who still bore a stern expression. "Perhaps—"

Graham stepped close, keeping his voice low and only between them. "I must advise you to take care, my lady. A knight with such a brutal past and fearsome reputation might be unstable."

Marian bristled at the accusation but maintained her decorum. "You are kind to be concerned for my welfare, my lord."

"I care for you, Marian. Truly. You must know this?" His expression softened, resuming a radiant glow as he smiled. "If we were to wed, this would all come to an end. I swear it."

"I…" Marian dropped her gaze, unable to find words. "You are too kind, my lord."

"Why do you resist?" He hooked a finger beneath her jaw and lifted her gaze.

It took all her effort not to jerk away from his touch, not to lash out. Instead, she demurred, taking a deep breath and studying his face. "I cannot marry you, my lord."

Graham's smile faltered, and again, a shadow returned to his eyes. "You love him."

The statement hung heavy in the air between them. Marian said nothing. 'Twas better for him to assume her love of another than to recognize her disgust at the thought of marrying him.

He leaned closer still. The bustle of movement in the bailey faded into the distance. The skin along her arms and neck prickled with unease, pebbling with gooseflesh. These words were solely for her.

"If you do not marry me, you and all you love will suffer." A feral grin replaced the kind smile she once admired. "I will slaughter everyone you hold dear. I will take your father's lands by force. Do not try my patience, sweeting. Marry me, and I will spare them."

"The king will never allow this."

"Who do you think the king will believe?" His grin remained. "I am his loyal subject, and you? You are but a woman."

"My father will hear of this. He will—"

"Your father?" Graham's chuckle left her cold and empty. "Your father is a step from death's door."

She could feel horror blossoming on her face and realized he could see it too.

"Aye, sweeting, I know the truth."

"You cannot do this." Her throat constricted. She wished for her dagger…one thrust and she could end this madness. Instead, she gripped her skirts, helpless as fury consumed her.

"I shall return on the morrow to speak with your father and make the proper arrangements."

"If you cross that threshold again, I will kill you myself." Marian held her chin high in defiance. "I would rather *die* than become your wife."

"That can be arranged," he said before sighing. "Pitiful waste. I had hoped to sample your delights…as the Grim Knight has."

She sucked in a breath and glared at him.

"I shall give you one day. If I hear nothing by midday tomorrow, then…well, you know the consequences." Graham stepped away and retrieved his mount.

As he rode through the gate with his small entourage following behind him, Marian craved the firm curve of her bow in her hand, the solid weight of an arrow, imagining it flying with ease to strike him in the heart. After the gates closed, she ran to the great hall, passing Captain William as he retreated to his quarters.

"Captain." She stopped him, resting her hand on his arm. "Under no circumstances are Lord de Bough or his men allowed inside this keep, am I understood?"

"As you command, my lady." He bowed and took his leave without question.

Marian raced up the stairs to Guy's quarters to find him unconscious. Her gaze drifted over his bare chest to the low drape of the bedclothes across his hips. "How is he?"

"Och," Anne tutted, working diligently with herbs to treat the wound on his side. "He will be hale and hearty after a good rest. Nothing but scratches and a blow to the head. Once I give him this tonic, he will be right as rain."

Marian sagged against the bedpost. He would recover. She feared what he would say—or do—when she relayed Graham's threat.

How could she have been so blind? Graham was behind it. Behind all of it. He did not want *her*; he wanted her father's estate. No matter the cost.

Chapter Eighteen

Guy struggled to tear himself free of the cloistering darkness. His lids felt weighted, and it was difficult to open them. Slowly, light filled his vision, blurry and disorienting. He blinked several times to clear the haze.

Flickering firelight played along the familiar stone walls of his chamber. A gentle trickle of memory filtered into his sluggish mind. Marian…the bastard traitor in the bailey…pain and darkness. He groaned as he attempted to sit up, his limbs useless on the bed. His legs refused to respond to his command. 'Twas as if his body had finally reached its limit.

"You should rest."

Such a sweet, familiar voice. A burst of agony echoed through his skull when he turned his head, searching the room for her. He pinched his eyes closed, ignoring the throbbing in his head. When he reopened them, Marian stood at his bedside, concern pulling her lips into a frown…or was it anger?

"Your concern touches me." He shifted, willing his body to move. It relented, but the effort left him aching. Finally propped up against the headboard, he studied her unmoving form.

"You could have been killed." She folded her arms across her chest. "The captain told me of your rash behavior."

"The reivers attacked." He shrugged one shoulder, and the movement made him moan. "Was I not upholding my part of our bargain?"

"At least killing yourself in such a manner would free me from my own obligation to that cursed bargain."

His lip curled in amusement. "Come now, vixen. You cannot have me believe you do not enjoy fulfilling your end of the agreement?"

Warmth painted her cheeks a lovely shade of rose. She glowered at him. "I should finish what they started."

He lifted empty hands. "I bear no weapon and am injured. I am at your mercy."

Marian scoffed. "Would you have me behave as you? Without consideration, showing no mercy, no conscience to your actions?"

"I would have you change nothing about yourself except the distance you keep between us." He crooked his finger to beckon her closer.

She cast her gaze to heaven and muttered under her breath. Taking several steps, she sat beside him at the edge of the bed and scowled.

"Much better." He relaxed, studying her lovely profile as he carefully selected his next words. "Graham de Bough is a traitor, to his neighbor and to the crown."

Marian's eyes widened, her lips pressed into a line, but she said nothing.

"You do not seem surprised by this revelation?"

"I suspected it, but when you returned, you threatened him, called him a traitor." She picked at her fingernail. "I watched him while you made these accusations. His expression faltered, and I could see the truth in that moment."

Guy tensed as though bracing for a blow. "What did he say?"

"He again requested my hand in marriage, which I rebuffed." She inhaled sharply before continuing. "This time he…he threatened me, should I not comply with his request."

Ignoring the pounding in his head, Guy leaned forward and took Marian's jaw in his hand, tilting her chin up. "What exactly did he say?"

"He vowed to kill everyone I loved should I refuse to marry him."

"Did anyone hear him make this threat?"

Marian shook her head, a tear slipping down her cheek. She angrily wiped it away. "When I proclaimed my outrage and told him I would take the matter to the king…well, he laughed. *Who would believe a woman?*"

"Fuck." Fury snaked through Guy, replacing the ache of

injuries. He would see the bastard whipped for his impudence. Then he would run him through with his own sword.

"What am I to do? I cannot allow him to bring further harm to the people I love." Her lower lip trembled, and he gently traced his thumb across it.

"Have you discussed it with your father?"

"Nay. 'Tis only my father's firm desire for me to wed Lord de Bough that kept him asking for so many years." She shrugged. "I fear there is no way to dissuade my father of the idea."

"Lord de Bough is the man responsible for the reiver raids. 'Tis by his order they target your father's lands."

"Have you any proof?" Marian glowed with hope.

"Only the rambling confession of a reiver I held beneath my blade." Guy swore again. "The bastard escaped when his companions regrouped and attacked."

"Is that how you ended up with this?" She touched the side of his head, and he winced.

"Aye. 'Twas fortunate the captain and his men arrived before the reivers could finish what they began." His body sagged at the memory. Never before had he been quite so vulnerable as he was in that moment. He loathed the idea of being in debt to Captain William, but if it were not for his quick thinking, Guy would be dead and all would be lost.

"'Tis possible my father will listen to reason if we convey this to him."

"And what will that do? He cannot petition the king—any message we send will be intercepted by Lord de Bough."

"God's blood, teeth, and bones." She frowned. "It is truly hopeless."

An idea formed in his mind. "Your father cannot bind you to another if you are already wed…"

"What madness do you speak?" Marian quirked a brow. "Surely, you cannot be proposing we wed?"

"I am."

"I have no intention of entering the institution of marriage…with anyone."

"We do not have to follow through with it. But if your

father believes we are already intimately acquainted, he will have no choice but to give his blessing to our union."

Marian's mouth fell open. "You wish to tell my father you have ruined me and wish to take me as wife to salvage my reputation?"

"Would you prefer to wed the traitor?"

Guy held his breath. She would never follow through with the ruse. No one would know it was a pretense to infuriate and draw out Lord de Bough.

"I would rather *die.*"

"When he learns of our engagement, he will show his true intentions, not only to your father but to the world. Especially if he follows through with his threats."

She tapped a finger along her jaw as she pondered the proposition. "Shall we tell my father of Lord de Bough's duplicity and of his threats?"

"Nay. The traitor will unveil himself and his true nature as soon as he hears of our union."

"Who will believe it?" Marian's brow furrowed. "Every servant in the keep and farmer in the barony has seen how we loathe one another."

Guy took her hand in his, trailing his fingertips along the inside of her wrist. She shivered at the touch.

"They see the truth, Marian. They see what we never speak aloud. The desires of our hearts."

"And what is the desire of your heart?"

Her breath caught when he brought her wrist to his lips, pressing them to the soft skin where her blood ran hot.

"You, vixen." He held her gaze, allowing the wall around his heart to crack and splinter. "From the first moment I saw you at court, I desired only to earn your favor, your trust…your heart."

She blinked, her plush lips parted, her hand trembling. "Why?"

"I have never met a woman with such passion and loyalty. You are stronger than soldiers I have bested on the battlefields. Wiser than leaders who charge me. You love deeply, fully, and without hesitation. I have seen the pride you take in caring for those who cannot care for themselves." He licked his lips, uncertain of this confession, but he blundered forward, unable to stop.

"In all my years, I have served myself first and foremost. The years of hunger, pain, and torment would have been easier if there had been someone who cared for me as you care for your people."

Tears spilled down her rosy cheeks. She cupped his face in her hands. "I thought the Grim Knight showed no mercy?"

"You have heard the truth behind my exploits as the Grim Knight and know there is more to me than the darkness of those tales." He pressed his hands over hers. "I will not hold you to our arrangement, Marian. Once we expose de Bough, I will release you from obligation."

Surprise lit her eyes.

"You do not wish to wed, and I shall not force your hand."

"What of the…other bargain we struck?"

"Have you not wondered why I have not taken you fully?" He kissed her palm. "I crave you. Night and day. You torment me. I long for nothing but to bury myself in you, to bring us both unspeakable pleasure."

A soft gasp escaped her.

"But if I have you, Marian, I will have *all* of you. Body and soul. With you as my wife." He growled at the hunger in her eyes even as the same gnawed relentlessly at him. "I will not settle for merely a taste to sustain me throughout my life. There are no half measures here."

"I understand." She withdrew her hand and sat back. "I should speak with my father."

Disappointment crushed him at her easy dismissal of his passion, but he would dwell upon it later.

"Are you well enough to accompany me?" She stood and smoothed her hands over her skirts. "'Twould be best if the announcement came from a united front."

With a groan, Guy pulled himself to the edge of the bed. "Help me." The words broke from his lips without shame. If he could trust anyone, it was her. The only threat she bore was to his heart.

Marian took his arm to steady him as he stood. "Can you manage?"

"Aye." He rested his hands on her shoulders and met her concerned eyes. "With you by my side, I can fight the entire continent."

Her soft chuckle rippled through him, warming him. She helped him dress, took his arm, and led him to the door, to her father.

He prayed their ruse would be convincing. They played with fire, and Lord de Bough would burn them all to the ground if they were not careful. All they had to do was draw out the traitor, hunters luring in their prey.

But Lord de Bough was no simple quarry. He was a wolf masquerading as a sheep, ready to strike in retaliation should they attempt to take what he believed to be his.

The hunt was on.

Chapter Nineteen

I crave you. Guy's words rang clear in her mind. *If I have you, Marian, I will have all of you.* His confessions were not ramblings but detailed assertions, as though he had pondered them through many a sleepless night.

She had been wrong. Her first impressions of Sir Guy Silverthorne had been shattered in the wake of their time together. He was no longer a specter of terror encompassed by the horrifying past of the Grim Knight. This man was far more complex. And he desired her—body and soul—for *his* bride.

In the corridor outside her father's chambers, a sense of calm certainty shrouded her. Where there should have been outrage within her heart of hearts, she felt only a peaceful nudge toward the path leading to him.

He paused beside her, and her cheeks warmed at his proximity, plagued by the memory of his honest admissions.

With an affirming nod, she knocked on the chamber door.

It swung open, startling her with the abrupt response. Anne's dour face filled her vision. Her heart pounded, fear choking her.

"Is he…"

Anne shook her head. "Nay, but he feels rather poorly today, my lady."

"May we speak with him? 'Tis of great importance."

With a sigh, Anne stepped aside and opened the door to admit them.

Marian led the way into her father's dim chambers. The curtains, drawn against the daylight, cast the room into shadow. The warmth from the fire filled the space, and a bead of sweat formed on her lip.

Guy remained by her side as they approached the bed. With his lips pressed tight together, he surveyed the room and the occupant lying under dark bedclothes.

Her father seemed a ghostly shell of the man she had always known and admired with such ferocity. He lay still, his eyes closed, his hands clasped in his lap. For a brief moment, she believed him to be dead, stolen away without word or warning. A sob caught in her throat.

"Marian, is that you, child?" Her father's raspy voice silenced the fear, and she smiled, reaching out to take his extended hand.

"'Tis I, Father." She sat on the bed beside him and cradled his hand to her chest, stroking the fragile skin.

The baron's misty gaze shifted from her to the man standing tall and broad beside her. "Sir Guy." He coughed, a heavy, rattling sound, and sighed. "Has something happened?"

"Well…" Marian's courage failed. She'd intended to tell her father everything. Of the reivers, of the plot set into motion by Lord de Bough, someone whom her father believed to be a friend and ally. But seeing him in this weakened state broke her resolve. Nothing would be gained from telling him. 'Twould only agitate his condition, and he would be unable to do anything in retaliation. The shock alone could kill him.

Marian looked at Guy. A flicker of understanding passed between them.

"I have come to ask for your blessing, sir." Guy stepped closer, ensuring his words were clear and strong. "I wish to wed your daughter."

The baron's bushy brows rose, disappearing beneath his cap. "You wish to wed Marian?" A soft chortle rumbled his breath. "You are a braver man than I."

Marian and Guy exchanged another look at her father's unexpected reaction.

"This is quite surprising." The old man sobered, his gaze alternating between them for a long moment. Eventually, he smiled at her. "I must confess, I had long hoped to see you wed before I passed, my dear. Your personal convictions against marriage made finding a suitable partner quite challenging. I had hoped you would wed Graham to unite our families."

She bit her tongue to keep from unleashing a torrent of curses and spilling the truth of the traitor to the east. Guy rested a hand on her shoulder, a comforting touch that grounded her.

"I have had time to consider all possibilities, Father." She lay her cheek against Guy's hand, and in response, he stroked her jaw with his thumb. Warmth bubbled inside her at the simple touch. "Sir Guy has proven himself to be a fearless warrior and a loyal knight. It would be an honor to be his wife."

The words were an act, a means to placate her father's dying wish to see her settled, wed, and safe. But even as she spoke, they rang with a truth echoing deep in her bones. Being his wife would be an honor…and an endless pleasure. She could not bring herself to meet his gaze, not while her body trembled and her heart pleaded with her mind to embrace this man who saw her as the treasure she was.

"I do not know how you convinced my stubborn, lovely daughter to enter into such an arrangement," the baron said with a toothy grin. "But I see no reason to deny your request for her hand in marriage. You have my blessing. I pray you both find peace and joy in your union."

Marian pressed a kiss to her father's hand as her tears fell free. He wiped them away and drew her close, kissing her forehead.

"I love you, Marian." His eyes shone with pride and unshed tears. "I only wish I could live to see my grandchildren."

With a laugh, she shook her head. "Is it not enough to see me happily wed, Father?"

"I would see your house overrun with bairns." He chuckled again. "Your mother would be proud of the fearless woman you have become."

Marian blinked away tears. "I love you, Father." The words caught in her throat, stealing her breath, pressing heavily on her heart.

"Go. Begin preparations for your wedding. I wish to rest so I may celebrate with you."

Rising from her seat, Marian paused and leaned down. With a soft kiss to his temple, she murmured a prayer for protection and serenity for her father. She was not a pious woman and put little stock in religion, yet what harm could it do to give them all peace of mind?

As she turned toward the door, the baron's voice echoed behind her. "Sir Guy, I would have a word with you in private?"

"As you wish, my lord." Guy paused halfway to the door and met her curious gaze.

She melted at his lopsided smile and took his nod for the dismissal it was.

When she closed the door behind her, she found Anne standing outside the door, her hands propped on her ample hips.

"Is it true then?" Anne asked, her eyes wide, her lips pursed.

"Can I not have a single conversation within these walls without someone overhearing it?" Marian sighed in exasperation, but a smile slowly broke free.

She only had a moment to be stunned by Anne's brilliant smile before the stalwart maid threw her arms around her. "Oh, my lady, I must confess my relief."

"You were concerned of my fate should I remain unwed?" she teased her friend.

"Not in the slightest." Anne dropped her voice so it carried only between them. "But what would happen if you should conceive a babe out of wedlock with the handsome knight? The whispers are bad enough."

"Anne, what do you speak of?" Confusion tangled in her mind, even as her cheeks warmed with shame at being caught. "What whispers?"

"My lady," Anne tutted. "You said yourself, these walls hear *everything*."

Realization crept over Marian, painting her face red with embarrassment.

"The whole keep knows of your dalliances with the Grim Knight, my lady." Anne's kind smile soothed her as they walked to Marian's chambers.

"What do they say?" She lifted a hand to stop Anne from speaking. "Nay, I do not wish to know."

"'Twas evident the moment you both rode through that

gate." Her maid chuckled. "The two of you fighting at every turn, eyes flashing, teeth bared. Such passion cannot be contained."

"Oh." Marian waved her hand, but the observation struck a chord within her.

Anne took her leave as Marian closed her chamber door and leaned against it. The maid was right. From their first meeting, there had been something simmering between them. Hatred. Passion. Desire. Guy ignited these things deep within her, but now a new emotion churned, resplendent and glittering in the sun as she held it up to examine it.

Love.

Did she love him? She surely cared for him. Desired him. But love? What was love?

Marian pressed a hand to her fluttering heart and inhaled deeply to steady her breath. She waited for unrelenting panic to grip her at the thought of surrendering herself to Guy.

But it never came. Her thoughts and emotions flowed like a river through her, peaceful and serene, leading her to the answer she sought.

She *loved* the Grim Knight, Sir Guy Silverthorne, with all his wickedness, faults, and scars.

This night, she would surrender not only her body but her heart as well.

He would be hers as much as she was his.

Confident in this decision, Marian slipped from her chamber and sought refuge in his to await his return in naught but desire.

Chapter Twenty

The moment the door closed behind Marian, the air shifted in the baron's chamber, growing thick and heavy with unspoken words from the darkest reaches of his mind.

"What intentions do you have toward my daughter?" The baron's question was clear, cutting straight to the heart.

Guy turned to face him. "My lord?" He examined the man's face, finding curiosity etched beneath age and exhaustion.

"My daughter has always been as stubborn as an ass." He sighed. "I have never possessed the strength to deny her wishes. I fear it has ruined her."

"I disagree. Her spirit may be unconventional and misunderstood, but it has served her well."

The old man cocked his head. "You love her."

Guy made no attempt to deny it. It was not a question but a keen observation. Instead, he clasped his hands behind his back and nodded.

"I may be old and infirm, but I am not blind." He winked playfully, then sobered quickly. "The reivers…"

"My men will take care of the reivers, my lord," Guy said with certainty. Since he had uncovered the truth of their loyalty, 'twould be only a matter of time before it was tested…and broken.

"Lord de Bough will be displeased about your union with my daughter." The baron pressed his lips in a thin line. "You will be met with resistance once word of your marriage reaches him."

Pleasure ebbed through him at the prospect. "I relish any opportunity to show him exactly how little I truly care for his opinion."

The baron narrowed his gaze. "How now? Is there bad blood between you?"

"Aye, my lord. Traitors and cowards are not tolerated in my

presence."

"Mind your tongue, lad. Those are powerful accusations."

Guy cursed his slip of composure. Marian had chosen to keep the truth of Lord de Bough's betrayal from her father. He could not be sure whether it was out of concern for his failing health or to save him the shame of knowing he had supported their union, and in fact, encouraged it. It had been his intention to remain silent upon the matter, but now the words danced in the air between them. With a sigh, he relayed their discoveries, including the events of the last fortnight.

The baron blanched at the slow revelation. What began as denial transformed to disbelief as Guy revealed the duplicitous actions of their neighbor and ally. Rage deposited color in the baron's pale cheeks when Guy spoke of Lord de Bough's involvement.

When Guy revealed the threats spoken against Marian by one the baron trusted, her father snapped. "Enough!"

Guy fell silent.

After a breath, the old man shifted. "You have no doubt as to his involvement?"

"None, my lord."

"If this is true, your marriage will not go unchallenged." He studied Guy carefully, searching for weakness or hesitation. "Lord de Bough will come for you to retaliate. He has made no secret of his desire to wed Marian. He will see this as a slight against him. He will challenge you."

"I welcome the opportunity, my lord." Fire blazed within Guy at the thought of the arrogant curmudgeon possessing that which belonged to him.

"I see." The baron exhaled a shaky breath and relaxed against the bed. "I will not revoke my blessing. You will be wed as soon as possible."

"May God grant you mercy, my lord." Guy bowed low before taking his leave.

"Sir Guy." The baron's broken voice echoed through the room. "Protect her with your life."

"I shall. You have my vow." He pressed his hand to his

heart, ignoring the ache burning in his chest.

Guy passed Marian's maid in the corridor as she returned to the baron's chamber. His head pounded with the injury he'd sustained, but he could not bear the thought of remaining abed while Marian laid plans for their wedding…for their trap.

He twisted through the corridors. Where in the devil was she? He searched all the rooms within the keep and even walked the grounds. There was no sign of her, and everyone he asked had not seen her since morning. How strange. Even her horse remained in the stables.

Inside the great hall, he retraced his steps to her chamber before returning to his own. Wherever she was, he would find her. And then punish her for driving him to such a state. He opened his chamber door, and the agitation boiling inside him vanished.

Marian lay upon his bed. Unclothed.

A gleam of the setting sun streamed through the solitary window, casting her in a radiant glow.

"I grew concerned at your continued absence." She slowly rose to her feet.

Guy leaned against the door until it closed, the latch falling into place. His heart raced, thundering against his ribs. The ache in his head dimmed as his cock hardened.

"What game is this then, vixen?" He grinned. "Do you seek to torment me?"

She walked the length of the bed, her hand trailing along the sturdy bedpost at its foot. Seeing her lithe body stripped of all trappings, laid bare for him…his mouth watered. The memory of her taste, her scent was nothing compared to this vision before him.

"I have come to fulfill our agreement." She leaned against the bedpost, watching him with eyes of flickering midnight flame.

"Marian." He swallowed, restraining himself, maintaining distance between them. "If I take you, there will be no other. You will be mine alone."

"And what of you?" She strode to him and trailed her

fingers along his jaw. "Will you not in turn belong to me?"

Need cascaded through him at her question. He licked his lips. Never before had he imagined himself bound to another. He had never considered it until this moment. Desire burst through the restraints holding him spellbound.

Guy grasped her by the waist, pulling her to him. "I will be yours, vixen, until my last breath."

She sucked in a breath. He kissed her and unleashed himself, knowing they would be irrevocably bound for eternity.

Marian's lips parted beneath his as he plundered her mouth. She wrapped her arms around his neck.

He tasted her, savoring her heat and the soft mewling sounds of pleasure escaping from deep within her.

The dam inside him burst. His fingers threaded through her silken tresses. She tipped her face up, opening for him, clinging to his shoulders.

Gently, he broke the kiss and held her still while he caught his breath.

"I waited long for this moment. I will not take you like some rutting beast."

She bit her kiss-swollen lip. He admired the rose hue staining her cheeks, trailing down her neck, across her breasts.

"On the bed, vixen." With a small pout, Marian drew away and retreated to his bed. He glimpsed the glistening folds between her thighs as she climbed onto the worn counterpane.

He hungered for her. Ravenous, the beast he had been restraining growled inside him, desperate to devour all of her.

Guy stalked the length of the room, aware of her gaze upon him. He divested his doublet before sitting by the fire to remove his boots. When he stood and pulled the remaining garments from his body, heat consumed him.

Marian's lust-filled eyes trailed over his form. She sat on the bed, unmoving as he joined her. He prowled forward on his hands and knees, and she sank down, her hair splaying beneath her head, a dark halo against the red fabric.

Guy trailed his hand along the inside of her thigh, gently nudging her legs apart. He drank in the sight before him. Her skin kissed by the dying sunlight, flushed pink as a spring rosebud. The rise and fall of her breasts with each breath. He wanted nothing more than to bury himself inside her, to lay claim to her at last.

His fingers trailed along the crease of her thigh, brushing the downy thatch of hair.

A moan broke from her lips.

He covered her, his mouth to hers, his body over hers. Her sweet arousal teased his senses as he rocked himself against her, his cock sliding along her slick cunt.

"Take all of me, my Grim Knight." She nipped at his lip and arched her hips against his. "This is my surrender."

"As it is mine." He fit his cock to her and thrust.

A strangled cry ripped from her, and he swallowed it with a passionate kiss. Seated fully inside her, he stilled, needing more but aware of her discomfort. With every caress of his tongue, tension eased from her.

When she writhed against him, he indulged her, moving his hips to withdraw. She met each stroke with a gentle rock of her hips. The sensation drove him mad with desire. He gripped her tight, quickening his pace, thrusting harder and harder. She clung to him, clutching his shoulders, her nails digging into his flesh.

He ground his hips to hers, desperate to be closer, deeper. To be so entwined with her, he could lose himself only to be reborn by pleasure consuming them both.

Marian's breath grew ragged.

Guy fought his own release and pulled back. She whimpered at the loss of him. He sank down and drew her hips up until she blossomed for him, glistening with need. The first swipe of his tongue across her center tasted like pure heaven.

He feasted upon her as a man starved. When she bucked against his hold, he redoubled his attention until she cried out his name, her release sweet on his tongue.

Rising up, he fit himself to her again and drove himself to abandon. Her cunt pulsed around his cock, and he braced himself as he found his release. All thought fled as he filled her, blissful pleasure dragging them both under.

Nothing existed beyond her and him and this.

He kissed her forehead and leaned back to admire her beautiful, sated glow.

Marian smiled. A sincere, warm expression so lovely, it broke his heart.

"You belong to me now."

"And what will you do now that you have me, vixen?"

She reached between them, her fingers gliding over their combined release to grip the softening length of him. He gasped at her bold touch, his body responding to the curious way she explored his cock. It hardened, demanding more.

"I shall spend all night exploring your body." She nudged him down on the bed and disentangled herself from his limbs. When she straddled his thighs, he nearly expired at the sight of her swaying breasts, the rosy tips pulled tight.

"I am at your mercy, my lady." He grasped her hips and moved her against him, allowing her cunt to tease the length of his cock.

She tutted and pulled away.

He frowned and rose up on his elbows, watching as she shifted lower on the bed. A groan ripped from him when she wrapped her hand around his cock and lowered her gaze to study it.

"Does it bring you pleasure?" she asked.

"What?" He gritted his teeth against the sensations coursing through him.

"My touch."

"Aye." He tensed as she bent forward, bringing her mouth dangerously close to his cock.

"And what if I do this?" She held his gaze as she ran her tongue along the ridge of his cock.

"Fuck." The word ripped from him as she took him in her mouth. *I surrender.*

Chapter Twenty-One

Guy's satisfied groan echoed around his chamber walls. He arched his back, pressing his hips into the bed as she drew her tongue over his length, fisting his into the linens. A stuttered breath escaped him. She took him deeper, letting the head of his cock touch the back of her throat.

"Vixen," he gasped between breaths.

Marian preened at his reaction. Never before had she imagined the amount of power wielded by such intimate action. She savored every moan and shudder as she teased him, testing different pressures and techniques until he squirmed.

The sticky sweetness of his release, mingling with hers, lay heavy on her tongue. When her teeth scraped sensitive skin, he swore, cursing the sun, moon, and sky before leveling her with a stern, hooded gaze.

"Am I causing you pain?" she asked, pausing her ministrations to smile, her hand wrapped around his thick length.

"Fuck, my darling vixen. Your wicked mouth torments me."

"Shall I…" She released him and drew back.

He growled deep in his throat and slowly rose. Marian scrambled backward with a soft laugh, edging just out of reach.

"Come here." He followed her every movement, his emerald eyes glinting in the flickering light.

Marian slid from the bed, her heart racing, her thighs slick. This is what she craved, the chase, the thrill of the hunt.

Since their first meeting, hunger had echoed inside her. At first, she mistook it for distaste, for the need to be away from him. Then the slow growth of their partnership blossomed, revealing the truth. She desired not only *him* but the pursuit.

Graham may have pursued her hand, but he had never laid siege to her heart. None had ever attempted to reach beyond the veil to understand her, to seduce her. Not as Guy had done.

Even now, he watched her every move like a wolf stalking its prey. On his hands and knees, he crawled toward her, his muscles stretching taut beneath his skin. He climbed from the bed, lowering his feet to the floor.

Marian licked her lips, her limbs trembling, poised for his strike.

"You cannot flee, vixen." His lips curled in a devastating, feral smile. "You are mine, and I fully intend to ravish you until dawn breaks the horizon."

"Ravish me?" A breathless laugh escaped her even as her heart fluttered in response to his admission. "Methinks you are mistaken."

"Did you not vow to be mine with your surrender?"

"As did you," she countered with a smirk, stepping close to him and tracing her finger over his heart.

Guy tensed, his naked form a statue carved of warm muscle and bone. She savored the rapid beat beneath her hand when she pressed her palm to his chest.

"Aye." His voice hummed through her, and he rested his hand upon hers. "Ravish is too tame a word for what I wish to do."

Marian's breath caught in her throat as he pulled her flush to him, his cock nudging her hip, his breath teasing her ear.

"I will worship you with my mouth, my hands, my cock." His tone rumbled like a storm gathering on the horizon. "I intend to defile you in ways you cannot imagine. Pleasure will be your constant companion. If I had my way, we would remain abed for a week. Even then, I would not tire of your body, of your presence. You are my goddess, my salvation, my love. I crave you with a ferocity I cannot comprehend."

Her body thrummed with delight at his words. She pressed herself closer, twining her arms around his neck. His confession resonated within her, mirroring her own desires. The desperation terrified her, but she clung to him, knowing they would drown together because he would not abandon her.

"You torment me in every possible way, vixen." He buried

his face in her neck and inhaled.

"So you keep telling me." She trailed a fingertip along his jaw.

He snatched her wrist and brought it to his lips. Her legs shook, nearly giving out beneath her. His tongue trailed over the delicate skin. Heat pricked at her as desire slowly rose.

"Place your hands on the bedpost." He released her wrist and stepped back.

She swayed at the sudden loss of his solid body.

Guy stood patiently, his hands at his sides.

Marian swallowed a sharp retort and reached for the bedpost, placing her hands on the solid, carved beam at the foot of his bed.

"Mmm…" His approval rippled through her like a dram of warm mead. "Spread your feet wider."

Heat speared through her as she obeyed. Cool air touched her wet center. Boldly, she met his gaze as he finished his slow appraisal of her bare length. She wiggled her hips, and he sucked in a breath between his teeth.

Guy closed the distance between them and palmed her breasts. He held the weight of them, squeezing, pulling her nipples between his thumbs and forefingers. Marian nearly sagged against him, and her hands slipped from the post.

"Grip it hard." He placed her hands back on the wood before resuming his slow exploration of her body. "Do not remove them. Understood?"

"What are you…?" Her question dissolved into a gasp as he cupped her sex. His fingers slid through her swollen, slick folds. She moaned, allowing sensation to carry her away.

Soft, teasing touches left her trembling. He ran his lips over her shoulder, nipping at her neck, at her ear as he stroked her. Panting gasps filled the air, surrounding them with a haze of desire.

"Guy, I beg you…" She licked her lips, digging her fingernails into the wooden post.

He rubbed his cock on the cleft of her ass, grinding against her, teasing her cunt with his blunt fingertips. Arousal coated his hand and her thighs. She arched her back against him. His cock brushed her sex, making her whimper. He angled himself enough to slide into her, fulfilling her wordless plea.

"Saints." She stilled at the thick fullness of him.

Guy moved, rocking his hips, thrusting from behind as he continued his teasing touches.

Marian gripped the bedpost tighter, sensation threatening to overwhelm her. He slowly increased his pace until he was fucking her with abandon.

Her measured breaths shattered along with her sanity.

When she reached her peak, she closed her eyes, panting, whimpering. Flashes of firelight and embers sparked behind her lids. The force of it left her weak, and her legs buckled like a newborn foal's.

Guy scooped her into his arms and lifted her, boneless and sated, against him. She blinked up at him.

He laid her on the bed and pressed a kiss to her forehead before stepping away.

"Where are you going?" she asked, reaching for him.

"I am going to fetch some food before devouring you once more." He grinned. "I cannot ravish you on an empty stomach."

With a laugh, she waved him off. He drew on his hose and a tunic before retreating from the room. Marian closed her eyes, listening to the crackle of the fire and the steady beat of her own heart.

She remembered the first thought she'd had when she saw him. It had been pure lust. A spark of desire so sharp, so insistent, she refused to allow it to take any foothold, squashing it beneath her boot. The desire remained but was now warmed and mulled with spices and mutual understanding, intoxicating her. She craved more.

She could never have imagined such an improbable match. The Grim Knight was a bedtime story, a legend to terrify children into compliance and enemies into acquiescence. He himself admitted he was neither a good nor honorable man, and yet at every instance, he had proven himself to be all of these things and more.

The complexity of both his darkness and his light created a complicated display of shadow upon the walls of her heart. They eroded her barriers, tearing down the stone fortress she built around herself.

No man could compete with him. Guy stood with her. Even with his wicked bargain, he showed respect for her choice. There was always a choice. He demanded nothing she did not willingly share while defending her home, her family, and her people as though they were his own. She loved him for it.

Her eyes drifted closed as she waited for his return, replaying their lovemaking in her mind as she sank into blissful rest.

"Marian." The soft cadence of his voice pulled her from her sleep.

She blinked, finding Guy lying beside her, his face deep in shadow.

"I must have fallen asleep." She smiled, stretching out her arms and reaching for him. His eyes closed as she cradled his cheek in her hand. "Is something wrong?"

He inhaled deeply before opening his eyes. Pain flashed in their depths.

Marian scrambled to sit up.

Guy rose to sit beside her on the bed. He wore his tunic, doublet, hose, all perfectly set. She crossed her arms over her naked breasts. Something had happened.

"What is it?"

"Marian." Agony etched his handsome face, as though the words burning in his mind physically pained him. "Your father is dead."

Emotions cascaded through her like a waterfall—disbelief, uncertainty, fear, followed by a crushing weight of guilt and grief.

She wrenched herself from his hold when he tried to comfort her.

Her father, Jonas Ravenwood, Baron Ravinell. The man who raised her, who loved and supported her.

Gone. Dead.

Agony pierced her heart, shattering her completely,

breaking free in a scream that shook the keep.

Chapter Twenty-Two

By the time they had dressed and stood outside the baron's chamber door, unease had settled around them. Given their brief conversation with the baron the prior evening, they'd had no indication of his imminent passing. If anything, their interaction had shown him in good spirits and determined to see his daughter wed.

And yet, they woke to find the baron deceased, casting the occupants of the keep into turmoil and grief.

Guy reached for her, resting his hand on her shoulder. When she turned, her eyes glistening with tears, sorrow carved on her lovely face, the weight of it all crashed down on him. He stepped close, standing steadfast behind her, and she leaned into him. Together, they would confront whatever lay before them.

Anne opened the door, her eyes red and puffy. "Och, lass…" Her voice broke, revealing a hint of Scots accent.

Marian stumbled into her open arms, and they retreated into the baron's chambers.

Guy lingered behind, allowing the women to grieve in peace. While he had not known the baron long and there was little he could say to offer comfort, he felt the loss keenly. Marian's sire had brought her up in a world where her strength and independence made her a target. Yet he followed his heart and raised a daughter worth more than all the jewels in Christendom.

His heart ached at the sight of the old man lying in the same position as the night before. Yet now, the eerie stillness of death hung in the room like a wet shroud, suffocating and stifling. Candlelight fell across the baron's pale face and blue lips.

Guy had encountered death multiple times over his life, but never was it this…peaceful. Blood and gore. Decay and rot. Those, he could bear. This, however, left his stomach roiling.

Why, he could not say. Perhaps it was the effectiveness of death's visit that left him uneasy.

Marian's sobs echoed around the solemn chamber as she approached the bed with Anne by her side. She traced her fingers over his face, committing his features to memory with her gentle touch.

"Father."

Her single word struck Guy's soul, fracturing it with the agony of her grief.

Pressing his lips together, he stood at the foot of the bed, watching in silence. He tempered his own rising emotions, his desire to comfort Marian, his mounting fury at the ill-conceived timing. Perhaps there was nothing foul at play, merely the will of God taking the baron in His time. And yet, he could not shake suspicion gnawing at his conscience.

"Anne?" Marian's soft murmur cut through his thoughts. "When did you last speak with him?"

"I brought him wine before I retired for the night. He seemed in good spirits after you visited him." She bowed her head. "When I returned several hours later, he was gone."

Marian's fingertips traced once more over his blue lips. "What wine?"

"The baron's favorite mead from a neighboring village." Anne smiled softly at the memory. "He indulged in a glass every eve before he slept."

"Did you pour the drink yourself?" Marian asked, her voice growing stronger.

"At first, aye. But as the baron took to his bed, the servants would have it already prepared when I entered the kitchen for his evening tonic." Her face blanched as she pressed her hand to her heart. "Saints preserve me! Do you believe…?"

"I believe my father was killed, yes." Marian turned to Guy, her eyes blazing with the promise of retribution. "Poisoned with nightshade or another herb to weaken his frail constitution."

"How can you be certain?" Guy asked, resting his hand on the hilt of the dagger at his hip.

"He had been ill for so long." Marian sighed. "There would

be brief moments when he would improve, only to be struck down within days, taking to his bed, unable to leave this chamber."

"There was no indication of poison at the time, my lady." Anne's eyes were wide. "And yet, looking back on it now…it could be possible."

"Not *possible*. It is evident." She took her father's frail hand in hers. "My father was slowly poisoned."

"Who would do such a vile thing?" Anne asked, horrified at the thought.

Marian turned to Guy, who straightened under her gaze. "Would he resort to murder?"

The slow unraveling of possibilities gave him pause, but he nodded. "He has gone to great lengths to push you in his direction, Marian. When you denied him, he threatened you. Murder is not beyond his capabilities."

"There is not a soul who will believe it. Not for a moment."

Guy lifted a shoulder. "Then we will have to draw a confession from his own lips."

"It will be our word against his. He will retaliate against such an accusation."

"Then we will set a trap."

Marian bit her lip, hesitating before speaking again. "I fear if we confront him, we will fall into a trap of *his* making."

"We will let him come to us."

Her eyes widened before she nodded. "So be it."

"I shall alert my men."

"Very well." Marian turned back to the baron. "I shall tend to my father."

Guy longed to cross the room, to take her into his arms to kiss her weary brow. Instead, he took his leave, allowing the two women to care for the baron.

With every step, his certainty grew. Lord de Bough had played a part in this, and he would uncover the truth should it cost him everything. After the man's threats to Marian, Guy wanted to dismember the bastard. De Bough's coercions had left the woman he loved shaken and furious. And while Marian was a woman of passion, she maintained a tact and diplomacy befitting her station. Guy held no such compunction for propriety or pleasantries.

When the bloody traitor returned, he would meet the tip of Guy's blade. There would be a confession and a reckoning.

In the bailey, Guy felt the shift in mood. Servants clustered together, whispering, casting uneasy glances around, their faces carved with grief and fear.

He spied Captain William leaning against the post outside the stables.

The man straightened as he approached.

"Sir Guy." He lowered his voice. "Is it true?"

Guy scouted his surroundings ensuring they were alone. "Aye. The baron is dead."

"May God grant him mercy." The captain crossed himself. His gaze narrowed as Guy remained silent. "Was his death…"

"'Twas murder, Captain. The baron was poisoned." He struggled to keep his tone low and even. Rage burned hot beneath his calm I. "There is a traitor in our midst. Someone who has access to the kitchens."

"I shall make inquiries."

Guy grabbed the captain by the wrist and pulled him to a halt. "Mention nothing of the manner of the baron's death. Out of respect for Mistress Marian in her time of grief, I wish to keep the matter quiet. Make your inquiries but keep them inconspicuous."

"As you wish." The captain bowed low, but when he rose, he lingered.

"Is there something you wish to share, Captain?"

"No, sir." He bowed to Guy and retreated toward the barracks, where soldiers sat in the morning sun.

Guy pondered the current situation. While he could not fathom the depths of Marian's pain, he could alleviate the pressure by unveiling the murderer. Part of him desired nothing more than for the pompous Lord de Bough to show his traitorous face.

Instead of remaining outside the stables, Guy walked the

perimeter of the bailey before climbing to the path along the stone battlements, scanning the horizon. When he encountered anyone, he spoke to them, inquiring as to their duties and marking their name. This garnered some uncomfortable conversations, since most of the keep's occupants viewed him as only the Grim Knight, a merciless wraith of legend.

After several hours, he grew weary. The sun stood at the highest point in the sky, and his skin prickled in the heat. He wiped his brow of sweat, then shielded his eyes against the light. Perhaps he should seek out Marian. She deserved to be part of this hunt for anyone played a role in the baron's death.

Guy noted the familiar figure of Anne crossing the bailey, heading for the gate. He saw no sign of Marian and frowned. Following his heart, he climbed down the nearest ladder and remained in the shadow of the wall as he made his way toward the great hall.

Inside the cool confines of the oversized room, he found Marian seated at the table where her father had regularly sat. She looked up as he approached. The tears had dried, but her eyes were rimmed with red and color stained her cheeks.

"I have spoken to the captain. He has things well in hand. No one will approach the keep without his knowledge." Guy sank down to the chair beside her.

"I sent Anne to the village to fetch supplies…to prepare…" Her voice caught in her throat, choking on the words.

Guy took her hand in his. He had no word of comfort, nothing more than his steady presence.

"I should have…"

"There are always things we *should* have done." He lifted her fingers to his lips and kissed the tips. "You cannot dwell upon these things. Your people need your strength, your courage."

"I cannot tell them how he died. 'Twould be a blight upon his memory."

"They deserve to know the truth." He spoke softly. "They may help us uncover the murderer."

At Marian's trembling nod, he stood. "Come. Let us take a turn in the garden."

She blinked up at him, her eyes bright, even through the sadness. "You wish to walk with me in the garden? What will they say of your fearsome reputation?"

"I care little for the opinions of others, vixen." He tipped her chin up. "So long as I am by your side, I am content."

Together, they strode to the exit, toward the warm embrace of sunlight, blue skies, and the subtle aroma of roses and herbs.

Halfway to the garden, they drew to a halt at the sound of shouting. Captain William raced toward them, his eyes fixed, his mouth set in a determined line.

"Lord de Bough is at the gate, my lady. Shall I admit him?"

Marian stiffened, her hand tightening in his. "Aye."

She and Guy shared a tense moment in silence to steady their thoughts and still their hearts.

"Come. Let us go meet the devil." Guy took a step, and she fell in beside him.

A small band of riders entered the bailey, parting to reveal the bastard upon a cream-colored gelding. He grinned as he approached, but his confident smirk faded when he beheld Marian's hand tucked firmly within Guy's. Fury flashed in his blue eyes before it melted into something sinister.

"I see you have made your choice, Mistress Marian." Lord de Bough dismounted with grace, and his men did the same, their hands resting casually on their swords.

"I have." She played her part with ease. "You are not welcome here, and yet, you have returned."

"Am I not allowed to pay my respects?" His wolfish grin returned.

"Respects?" she scoffed. "I require nothing more of you than your immediate removal from my presence."

"Your father's passing is unfortunate."

Marian inhaled sharply at this needling response.

Lord de Bough reached into his doublet and removed a roll of parchment. "But I have come to ensure his wishes are carried out quickly."

"State your purpose and be gone," Guy growled, leveling him with a glare.

"This is an agreement I made with your father to be carried out upon his death." Lord de Bough held out a parchment.

Guy snatched it from his hand and scanned the contents, his stomach souring. A knotted ball of dread formed in his gut. Marian took the parchment and read it, her face paling with every line.

"'If my daughter is unwed upon my death, she will wed Lord Graham de Bough,'" she read aloud before crumpling the parchment in her fist. "'Tis too late. My father granted his blessing for my union with Sir Guy Silverthorne before he took his final breath. This agreement is null and void."

Lord de Bough retrieved the crumpled parchment from the ground and smoothed it, appearing unruffled by her statement.

"If you have no other document to the contrary, this is a binding contract." He tucked it back into his doublet. "The king will agree."

"What will the king say when he discovers your traitorous plot and the threats you have made to his loyal subjects?" She faced him without fear, her back straight, eyes focused.

Pride welled within Guy at the sight of her taking a stand. His fearless lady warrior.

"The king will understand the steps I took to ensure your protection, my lady." His gaze turned to Guy. "The Grim Knight threatened and seduced you to steal your virtue and your lands. He convinced you of his love, only to kill your father, ensuring his position as your husband remain unchallenged."

"What nonsense do you speak?"

"This *knight*," Lord de Bough hissed the word as though it burned his tongue. "Is a traitor to the crown. He colluded with the reivers and set his sights on Mistress Marian and her ailing father, in order to position himself in their good graces to convince them of his loyalty. All while plotting to steal not only the baron's land, but mine as well."

Disbelief struck him like an arrow to the chest. He reeled, uncertain of his own reaction to the drivel spilling from this fool's mouth. He looked around the bailey.

A crowd had gathered, listening with eager ears and stunned

expressions. Their whispered conversation rose in pitch as the lying bastard took another breath.

"Lies," Marian spat, rounding on Lord de Bough. "Leave this place and do not return."

"Mistress Marian. You are distraught, confused, consumed by grief for your father's death, swayed by the dangerous charms of the Grim Knight." He held out a hand to her. "Allow me to offer my aid. Let me be your salvation."

She stepped back, pulling Guy with her. "I would rather die."

"Grief has stripped you of reason." Lord de Bough took a step toward her.

Guy drew his sword and leveled it at his heart.

A melody of swords singing from their sheaths filled the bailey, followed by gasps from the gathered crowd. Captain William and his soldiers took position behind them, their swords also at the ready. One misstep, and the cobblestones would be stained red with innocent blood.

Guy lowered his sword. "Leave. Now."

Lord de Bough lifted his hands and retreated. "Would you truly harbor a traitor and murderer who poisoned your beloved father?" His eyes twinkled, even though his face held pious concern.

The cursed bastard. He knew the baron had been poisoned.

He had set the trap. They walked directly into it. Fuck.

"I shall return on the morrow."

Guy watched the pompous ass mount his horse and lead his party out of the gate. The moment it closed behind them, Marian wheeled around, ignoring the gaping curiosity of her servants, and pulled Guy to the stables.

"What are you doing?" he asked when she stopped outside her horse's stall.

"We must leave. Now." Her jaw tensed, and even as she spoke, her voice faltered. "My father is dead. Graham has won."

"We can face him."

"He will kill us." She shuffled her feet. "Unless…"

"Unless what?" Guy took her shoulders and forced her to

face him.

"We must go." She met his gaze, her lip quivering. "I must speak with my men."

"Why such urgency?"

"Because there is no one else I can trust. We cannot let his threats stand."

Guy conceded, stalking to his horse's stall and saddling the beast. He retrieved a few items from his chamber as Marian did the same. When they slipped through the postern gate, Guy spied the captain atop the stone wall, watching them.

He waved, and Guy knew this would be the last time they would truly be free. For now, with their disappearance, they had all but admitted their guilt as traitors to the crown.

Chapter Twenty-Three

The burden of grief grew heavier with each step deeper into the forest. She wept, silently wiping away tears as they dampened her cheeks. Her disbelief and anger grew in proportion to the heartache in her chest.

Her father was gone, her inheritance stolen. Everything she loved…gone before she could even gain her footing and catch her breath. Inside her mind, she replayed Graham's accusations, his threats, their dire implications.

No one would believe the truth if it came from her. Lord de Bough was a baron in his own right, respected among the king's courtiers. If she challenged his statement of events, 'twould tip opinions in his favor, not only because of his sex but because he held power. Her focus had always been on her people and their needs, not on mingling at court and preening like a peacock.

Guy followed behind, his horse's heavy footfalls a comforting reminder of his presence. From the moment they left the confines of the keep where she had been raised, he lingered behind her, keeping watch with a diligence that allowed her to breathe through panic and confusion.

Graham had betrayed them. The accusations he hurled in the bailey in view of every servant and soldier alike haunted her. She had nearly scoffed at the ridiculousness of his assertions. He made it sound as though Guy were the villain of this farce, hellbent on seizing control of her father's barony and her virtue by force, coercing the king to send him here when the opportunity arose. In doing so, Graham reframed the conflict, placing full blame on her and Guy and granting himself a reprieve from suspicion.

Agitation seized her, and her mount danced beneath the aggressive tilt of her heels against his flanks. She eased the pressure and soothed him with a gentle pat. When they reached the cottage, she would clear her head of intrusive thoughts, and united once more with her men along with Guy, they could devise a way to unveil Graham's deception.

The villain in their midst bore a charming smile, a golden crown of curls, and a pair of eyes the color of a cloudless sky. Marian could not fathom the depths of depravity in one's soul to breach the bonds of friendship. An ally, once trusted and welcomed as warmly as blood kin, had turned upon them. And for what? Her father's land? Her hand in marriage?

Unease swept through her as a gentle breeze rustled leaves in the branches overhead. She clutched the reins tighter and urged the horse through the thickening foliage. A slow turn of her head eased her fears. Guy remained several paces back, his dark eyes fixed upon her.

They remained silent until the familiar shape of the cottage appeared through the trees ahead. She dismounted, noting the other horses in the small paddock behind the building. Guy came alongside her and slipped from his own saddle. She tied her horse to a tree and turned.

"Marian." Guy's voice wrapped around her heart.

She stopped and inhaled a deep, steadying breath.

When she faced him, he bore the vulnerability she had glimpsed the night before, when he took her in his embrace, in his bed, and unraveled her with pleasure. He opened his arms, and she fell into them, accepting his unconditional support.

Without a word, he pressed gentle kisses along her crown and across her brow. She sank into his warmth. Slowly, the tension eased, replaced with a bone-deep sorrow that threatened to drown her. A sob rose. Then another. She trembled with rage, even as the tears fell. Clinging to him, Marian grounded herself in this moment, in the knowledge nothing would ever be as it was.

"I can never go back." The realization spilled from her lips as it was etched upon her soul.

"We cannot." Guy stroked her cheek before tipping her chin up. Mirrored deep in those green eyes, she saw her own fear and uncertainty. But there was something more, something darker. Something shining with promise.

"What shall we do?" Marian asked, resting her hand on his chest.

"There are two paths before us." Guy paused as if contemplating his words. "We can fight or we can flee."

Marian blinked. "We have no army, no support. Who would join our cause? Within a fortnight, the king will not grant me audience after Graham's lies reach him."

"We have your merry men."

"My men are loyal and will fight should I request it of them, but I would rather die than willingly throw them into a pit of vipers."

"Why not ask them? Let them decide for themselves how they wish to serve you. If they would rather avoid this conflict, they are free to go and may God be with them."

"I do not want to ask them to endanger themselves. Not for me. Not now that my father is gone and my world has been ransacked and ruined."

Guy smiled, a sad sweetness behind it. "But you will cast yourself into the flame to rectify this injustice?"

"They have slandered your name and besmirched your honor. He must be exposed for the vile traitor he is."

He chuckled. "So fierce, to defend me."

"Is it not in my nature to defend those I love?"

"You love me?"

"Much to my dismay." Her body flushed in the heat in his gaze. Guy nudged her playfully. "I will not abandon you in this hour of turmoil."

"We could flee. Leave England. Perhaps escape to Meradin and start anew."

Marian shook her head. "Graham will not let this rest. He will hunt me down. He will finish what he started. He will take pleasure in it. And when he finds us, he will torture you, punish you for a murder you did not commit." She cupped his cheek. "He will kill you for loving me."

"Then let him come." His growl sent a ripple of possessive

pleasure through her. "I will see him impaled on my sword before I let him bring harm to you."

"We must stop him." Marian ignored the part of her that wanted to run, to flee with him, to never look back. "If he takes possession of my father's lands, my people will pay the price of his cruelty and selfishness."

"What do you propose?"

"Let us speak to my men. I do not want to ask for aid, but perhaps they can provide counsel."

"Very well." He stepped back, releasing her from his embrace.

She shivered at the loss of contact but straightened, channeling strength to bolster her failing courage. As she approached the door, it swung open, revealing Michael and John.

"My lady." Michael pushed the door open, and the two men stepped aside to let Marian and Guy enter the small dwelling.

Inside, Marian met the somber expressions of her once merry men, their faces cast in muted shades of sunlight and shadow. She saw their grief as clearly as she felt her own.

"We heard about the baron…your father," John said, stepping forward. "Our most heartfelt condolences, my lady."

"He was a good man. Such ill health—" Jack began, but Marian could not bear it.

"My father was murdered." Surprise lit their eyes. Marian inhaled deeply before pressing forward. "I spoke with him last eve, and when I woke, he was dead. His ill health was nothing more than slow poisoning."

Their soft curses filled the void.

"Lord de Bough has cast blame upon Sir Guy Silverthorne to free himself of suspicion." Her eyes narrowed as she looked at each of her men. "He has threatened not only Sir Guy but myself and has laid claim to my father's land through a false assertion that my father signed a betrothal agreement, binding me to him."

"Lies!" Michael shouted. Murmurs of agreement rose with his cry.

"Exactly. Which is why I require your counsel." She licked

her lips, uncertainty nagging at her conscience. "He will most certainly send messengers to the king very soon, if he has not already done so."

"We will stop them." Michael stood tall, offering their aid, and motioned to Jack.

"This will only prolong the inevitable." Marian sighed. "We must apprehend Lord de Bough and take him to the king before he can spread his lies. To do this, we first need evidence of his agreement with the reivers and his plot to consume the lands along the border."

"Such a task is impossible," Michael replied. "We are but a band of brothers, not a garrison of soldiers. We could not stop the reivers. We failed as spies. How could we infiltrate his keep and reveal his traitorous dealings? 'Tis an invitation for death."

"We must uncover his nefarious plot, reveal his treason. Only then will the people be free and order restored."

"Or I could just kill him," Guy offered.

All eyes turned to him. He leaned against the door, a force of unnatural calm. The Grim Knight held her gaze.

"That is not justice." Marian remained still, her heart thundering in her chest. "You cannot kill him."

"He ordered your father's death without hesitation." Guy inclined his head. "Why can you not do the same? Give the order. It will be done."

"I will not lower myself to his despicable behavior." She held her chin high. "I am no murderer. There will be justice, not bloodshed nor vengeance."

"Then you condemn us all," Guy replied simply.

She crossed the room, ignoring the men who surrounded her. Standing before Guy, she took a breath.

"Would you have me with blood on my hands?"

"If you wish to be free from this monster, you must seize the moment." His eyes sparkled with hatred. "He has hurt you. Threatened you. Terrorized your people. Then, as if to spite God, he lays claim to what is *mine*. I cannot allow such offense to stand unpunished."

His fierce words struck her heart with their possessive

passion. Even through her conflicting emotions, they further enflamed her love for him. She cleared her throat and suppressed the urge to touch him.

"I would have you bathed in righteous blood." Guy cupped her cheek in his hand. "He wronged you, and I would have it set to rights with his life forfeit."

She gasped and looked at her men. Their grim expressions resembled Guy's fierce passion. As she met each man's eyes, he nodded. One by one, they gave their support. Not only for her, but for Guy's assertion—Lord de Bough must pay for his treason with his life.

With a deep, cleansing breath, she faced Guy once more. "How do we breach the keep without sounding the alarm?"

"Leave that to me," Michael said. "We can easily get inside."

"Once we are inside, how do we keep Lord de Bough from fleeing?" Marian paced the floor. "If he knows we are there, he will have us killed on sight and run to save his own hide."

"There is no alternative." Guy rested his hand on her shoulder, making her pause. "I will go alone and face him. I am no threat to him surrounded by his guards and his soldiers."

"He will kill you." Marian grasped his doublet in her fist as panic seized her.

Guy shook his head and a sly smile curved his sensual mouth. "If he wishes to find his bride, he will listen to me."

Marian arched her brow, uncertain of this plan. "Very well." She released him. "We have until dark. Then we strike."

The small band of men gathered around her, and again, Marian embraced the bond of brotherhood formed by their loyalty. Even if this would be her last sunrise upon this earth, she would not allow Graham the satisfaction of victory.

He would die, and she would sacrifice all to ensure the world knew the truth of his betrayal.

Chapter Twenty-Four

The sun set at the western horizon, dipping low behind the trees. Firelight flickered from torches set along the stone wall of the traitor lord's keep.

Guy glanced over his shoulder at the receding tree line as he approached his enemy's lair. His vow to kill Lord de Bough echoed in his mind. He would avenge Marian and restore not only her honor but her inheritance. Even if it meant sacrificing his own life.

Marian and her men were secretly making their way into the keep while he approached the main gate. Attracting the traitor's attention would ensure the others could breech the walls without being spotted. He fully intended to ensnare Lord de Bough's curiosity, then drive his blade through the man's heart.

Nix danced beneath him, shuffling his massive hooves and tossing his head, almost as if he could sense the tension coursing through his rider. With a firm pat, Guy urged the stallion toward the gate.

"Who goes there?" The guards stood ready, one taller than the rest. His gaze focused on Guy.

"Sir Guy Silverthorne. The Grim Knight." He added his byname as an afterthought, hoping it would conjure the fearsome image these men held in their minds when they saw him.

The commotion upon the wall indicated an immediate response. He stood in wait as the portcullis rose, allowing him entrance.

A cluster of soldiers, nearly a dozen, rushed forward as he crossed into the bailey. They surrounded him, weapons drawn, faces grim.

"Have you come to surrender?"

The sound of Lord de Bough's voice set his teeth on edge.

Guy's grip on the reins tightened as the pompous lord stepped into view.

"I have come to negotiate on Mistress Marian's behalf."

"Such negotiation would include your surrender, of course."

"Will you discuss terms?" Guy bit his tongue, unable to respond in the manner he would prefer. His task was simple—infiltrate the keep and get close to Lord de Bough. Then permanently end his reign of terror with a single swipe of the blade.

"There is nothing to discuss. I have already sent word to the king of your treason and my impending marriage." Lord de Bough waved his hand. "Arrest him."

Guy grabbed the satchel hanging from his saddle and tossed it at the lord's feet.

"What is this?" De Bough recoiled at the bloody sack in the dirt.

"The head of the messenger you sent to London." Guy grinned at the look of horror blossoming across the face of each soldier. Their hands trembled, and their blades wavered.

Lord de Bough's confident smile melted into annoyance. "You truly are as merciless as they say."

"'Tis known far and wide, I am not to be trifled with." Guy sat tall in his saddle, resting his hand on the hilt of his sword. "My demands will be heard."

No reason to inform them of the truth of the messenger's demise. When they set chase, his skittish horse had thrown the poor man from his saddle, breaking his neck. Guy severed it merely to ensure the lord understood no message would be delivered to the king.

A muscle in the lord's neck twitched as his scowl deepened. Judging from the change in his demeanor, it seemed the message had been received and an impasse reached.

"Very well." Lord de Bough eyed him suspiciously. "Remove his weapons."

Guy eased himself from the saddle and relinquished his sword and dagger. The soldier's hands shook as he took the weapons before stumbling behind his comrades. Lifting his hands in supplication, Guy turned to face his unwilling host. Nix squealed and tossed his head as another soldier took him by the reins to lead him away.

With a whispered prayer of courage to bolster his resolve, Guy held Lord de Bough's amused gaze.

"Shall we?" He mock-bowed, gesturing toward the towering building.

Four guards took up the space around him as he followed Lord de Bough into his great hall. The tables had been removed and the room arranged as a throne room with an intricately carved chair placed on the dais at the far end of the room beneath a banner bearing the de Bough coat of arms—a silver dragon on a scarlet background.

Gone were the warm trappings that had surrounded them during the feast only a short time ago. The stark reminder of that night, of the lord's attentions upon Marian, left Guy with bitterness on his tongue and rage burning through his blood.

The guards took their posts, one at each corner, watching him with blades ready. He flexed his hand, wishing for his own blade, but he knew this was exactly what they had planned. With a steady inhale, he assessed his foe.

Lord de Bough lounged in an ornate chair, draping his arm over the curved rest. "Do you truly believe you have a right to negotiate, sir?" His lips curved in a sardonic smile. "You are a traitor to the crown. I will be hailed a hero for your capture, for freeing Mistress Marian from your vile clutches."

Guy struggled to maintain his composure. He fashioned his expression into bland distaste, unwilling to show a sliver of true emotion unless it furthered his plan. "And yet...'tis you who has conspired with the reivers to terrorize the people of this region."

"My agreement with the reivers has nothing to do with you."

"It has everything to do with me." He steeled himself and pushed forward. "Mistress Marian petitioned the king for aid, and I willingly agreed to take part. Aid that would not have been needed had you not betrayed her father."

"Her father and I had an understanding," Lord de Bough snarled. "Had he kept his word, I would not have been forced to find other ways to advance my plans for us."

"Unleashing the reivers?"

"Among other things." He tapped his fingers on the arm of the chair. "'Tis fortunate I have allies at the baron's keep."

"You poisoned him." Guy muttered the statement, as if just figuring it out, but knew full well the lord's guilt in the baron's demise.

"Well, not directly, but I gave the order." He leaned forward. "Not that you deserve to know my reasons or the depth of my plan, but since you will not see the sunrise…" His voice drifted into silence.

"Release me, you bastard!" A woman's voice rang through the hall.

Guy whipped around to stare at the open door to the bailey. Dread filled his heart at the sight of Marian between two soldiers, their grips tight on her arms. *Damn and blast!* Despair followed as her men were brought in behind her, one by one, their faces covered in dirt and blood. They pulled against their captors but relented when they saw Guy standing before Lord de Bough.

"Marian," Guy whispered, his heart shattering as she passed him. He reached for her, but a guard struck his arm with the hilt of a sword.

She writhed against their hold, but to no avail. When she came to a halt before Lord de Bough, she sagged back, desperate to be away from him.

He rose from his makeshift throne and stepped down. The soldiers stood still, holding Marian firmly between them.

"Thought you could outwit me, sweeting?" He hooked a hand around her arm and pulled her to him.

The soldiers fell back, leaving her in the lord's embrace.

Guy's blood boiled at the sight. The bastard's hands on Marian, the confident sneer on his lips as he drew her close. It took all of Guy's willpower not to lash out and end his miserable life with his bare hands. But the moment Marian's gaze met his, he stilled, clenching his hands in fists.

"The sooner you embrace the inevitable, the easier this transition will be," Lord de Bough purred, stroking her cheek.

Marian stiffened, her back as straight as an ancient oak. From this short distance, Guy could see her eyes flash with fire and her jaw clenched tight. He had challenged her enough to recognize the defiance rippling through her. Only a fool would push her beyond this point.

Lord de Bough's attention shifted from Marian to Guy. "Take one last glimpse of this jewel you once possessed. She belongs to me now, and I will ensure the kingdom knows it."

"May God have mercy on your soul, for the lady will certainly not go willingly." Guy smirked.

"There is no force upon this earth to move me." Her voice rumbled with menace. "I would rather die here and now than submit to you."

"What of your treasured knight?" The lord tightened his grip on her wrist, making her wince.

Marian turned to Guy; their gazes locked in silent understanding. He would gladly sacrifice himself for her. Better for them to die together than live a life of torment apart. At his nod, she relaxed.

"I see." The lord heaved a sigh. "Bring her in," he called to the guards.

Before he could turn, the door opened behind him, and Marian's strangled gasp pierced the silence. Two guards led Anne between them, her cheek bruised and a gash marring her forehead. Dried blood smeared her unbound, tousled hair.

"Forgive me, my lady." Anne cried as she fell to her knees before Marian. A guard placed the edge of his sword to her throat. "Forgive me." She sobbed harder.

Tears streaked Marian's face. "What have you done?" she asked her captor. "Release her. She is innocent."

"Is that so?"

Guy's skin prickled at the lord's laughter.

"Tell her," de Bough continued.

The guard pressed the blade firmly to Anne's neck, and she jerked at the contact. Her sobs faded as she inhaled and shook her head.

"Very well." Lord de Bough leaned closer to Marian, his lips a breath from her cheek. "Anne has been quite useful over the years. She has served me well."

"You lie." Marian's gaze remained on the kneeling woman, her lips trembling. "Anne?"

The servant turned her face to Marian, her body shaking. "'Tis the truth. I...forgive me. I beg you."

"Why?" The question lingered between them. Guy heard heartbreak in his beloved's tone.

"Her family long served mine before my father sent her to yours." Lord de Bough chuckled. "Did she never tell you? Pity."

"Enough of this farce," Guy growled, lunging for de Bough.

The guards surrounding him drew their swords, awaiting the order.

Guy stilled and swore.

"Did you never wonder how I knew of your father's health? Of his death?"

Marian's knees buckled, but he held her firm.

"Saints above." Guy cursed again, wanting to free her from this torment. The implication of those words hung heavy in the air. 'Twas by his order her father had been murdered, but it had been Anne who administered the fatal dose. Anne had been slowly poisoning him, slowly making him weaker and weaker until his body could no longer sustain it.

A woman in whom the baron and Marian had placed their trust had betrayed them in the most horrific manner.

"It cannot be true." Marian squeezed her eyes closed and shook her head.

"Oh, it is." Lord de Bough drew Marian closer to him, even as she struggled to maintain distance between them. Her hip grazed his as her hands pushed against his chest.

Guy averted his gaze, knowing he could not retaliate, not without endangering every person in the room. He would not make that choice for Marian when she'd already had so much stolen from her. Her mother. Her father. Her home. Her life.

All that remained were gathered here in this moment.

"If you do not acquiesce to my will, I shall remove what resistance remains. Your loyal men, your wicked knight. All that you love will be carrion for the crows." He wrapped his hand around her throat. "Should you persist in defying me, I will confine you to your chambers and claim my right by marriage. Your body belongs to me, and even though you sullied it with lust for him, I will wipe his touch from your memory while I fuck you night after night. You will bear my children and slake my every desire."

Fury pulsed in Guy's temples. He bit his lip to keep from lashing out in rage. The blood on his tongue further fueled his hatred. He longed for nothing more than to see the bastard burn in hell. So much so, he would gladly burn as well, so long as justice was served. His eyes burned as the lord's hand trailed down to grasp her breast.

Lord de Bough wrenched her face toward him and kissed her. She writhed against him, stilling only when his grip on her throat tightened.

A sound of pure animalistic rage ripped from Guy's throat. He charged forward, uncaring for the soldiers and their weapons. The first blow sent him to his knees. Another guard wrenched his head back with a fistful of hair, forcing him to look at the horror before him.

Tears streamed down Marian's face, as her mouth was plundered by unwelcome assault. She pushed against Lord de Bough, her desperate hands raking his broad chest.

The grip on Guy's head tightened. He groaned as pain snaked down his spine. Behind him, her men joined the fight, fury evident in their curses and shouts.

Marian's hand disappeared beneath de Bough's doublet, and as though doused with ice water, both went still. His vile mouth lifted from hers. Slowly, he stumbled back, snatching her wrist from beneath the fabric.

A dagger glinted in the dim light, blood dripping down the blade and coating her hand.

De Bough's eyes widened in disbelief, and the pompous lord tore off his doublet to reveal a dark red stain blooming across his pale tunic. He pressed his hand to it, staring in horror at the ruby blood as he drew it away.

"You…" He lunged for her, and without hesitation, Marian drew the blade across his neck.

"Speak no more," she muttered, stepping aside as he dropped to his knees, his hands clawing at his open throat. The gurgling and hissing of his final breath echoed in the stunned silence of the great hall.

Marian turned to face Guy before her gaze drifted to the twenty guards encircling her. In an instant, her men were upon the soldiers, holding them captive.

Guy seized upon his own captor's stunned surprise, spinning and knocking the sword from the guard's hand. He dropped to his knees and grasped the hilt. Rising, he drove it into the man's torso, blood gushing over his hands, before kicking him out of the way and wrenching the blade free.

Marian rushed to him, determination emblazoned on her lovely face. In a wordless understanding, she nodded, brave and unyielding. She spun, placing her back to his as the remaining soldiers rushed forward, blades drawn. Even with their master fallen, they stood their ground with misguided loyalty.

He gritted his teeth, bracing for battle. The pressure of her against his back emboldened him. He was more than capable of fending off the attack, but knowing she protected him as he shielded her spoke more than words ever could. The clang of their swords rang out in the chamber as the first wave crashed upon them, the sound echoing off timber and stone.

Bloodlust poured through him as he moved his sword with fluid purpose. His need for revenge, for absolution pulsed a war drum in his mind. Every hour of training in the lists, every encounter on the battlefield had prepared him for this moment. He embraced it, allowing the legendary myth of the Grim Knight's prowess to come alive to wreak havoc on his enemies.

Guy blocked oncoming blows, swinging his sword arcs, one after another, as two soldiers charged forward. He pushed them back with a shove and parried a third attack from his right. One man regained his footing, charging forward again. Guy's sword clashed with the oncoming blade, sliding to the hilt.

Their eyes locked, a grimace on the unyielding mouth of his opponent. A blur of scarlet from the corner of his eyes showed an impending assault from the left. But Marian, in a flash of emerald green, blocked the blow with her sword, and drove the attacker to the ground, impaling him with her blade. Then she vanished, returning to protect his back. He grinned as he turned again to his opponent.

The attacker pushed, catching Guy on weak footing for only a moment. He rebalanced, sliding against Marian. She caught his weight, bearing the brunt of his back pressed to hers. Her hand braced against his thigh for leverage. With a shout, he threw his weight forward, shoving his opponent and sliding the blade across his throat. The man stumbled and collapsed at his feet, blood spurting from the gaping wound.

The echo of battle raged behind him, but his focus remained on the men charging him, tripping over their fallen comrades, swords at the ready. He spun, drawing them away from Marian. The first soldier came quickly, and Guy parried with little effort before knocking him in the back of the head with his hilt.

Another ran forward, and Guy spun out of reach.

Two more flanked him. He stepped away from the carnage, leading them to level ground. Guy growled low, beckoning them closer with his bloody hand. They hesitated for a moment before attacking him simultaneously. With the ease of a well-practiced warrior, he stepped out of reach, disarming one before spinning and driving his blade into the other.

The first caught his balance and searched for his fallen sword. A well-placed kick to the knee sent the poor bastard to the ground. Guy rounded on him, blade to his throat, placing his boot upon another fallen man's chest as he attempted to scramble to his feet.

A wordless plea lit his eyes. Ignoring it, Guy plunged his sword into the soldier's heart and ripped it free, tearing chunks of flesh loose. Warm blood spattered across his face. His breath heaved as he surveyed the damage and braced for another attack.

But none came.

Silence fell around him like a shroud of darkness. The battle was over.

Guy turned at the gentle press of a hand on his arm, his sword still raised. But tension eased from him at the sight of Marian's beautiful face.

He caught her by the waist, hoisting her against him. She threw her arms around his neck.

"You *are* a great swordsman," she whispered in his ear.

A harsh laugh caught in his throat as he held her. "You sound surprised?"

Marian released him and took her place by his side. The remaining guards knelt before her three merry men, whose swords were still drawn and ready. Without their lord's protection, these men were at the mercy of the Grim Knight.

"What now?" Michael asked, his question directed at Marian.

Guy stood beside her, his gaze skimming her bloodstained face. He said nothing, only awaited her instructions. Never had he expected Marian to kill Lord de Bough. Taking a life had never been in her nature. Gratitude and pride filled him. Her actions ensured her survival…ensured *their* survival.

She met his gaze, her jaw steeled as she regarded him. Her attention drifted to a spot beyond his shoulder. He turned to see Anne on the floor, her eyes wide, her mouth open in silent protest. A blade lay beside her open palm, covered in blood.

"Damn." He knelt beside the woman and closed her eyes with a gentle brush of his fingertips.

Guy looked at Marian. Her face was a twisted tapestry of grief, shock, and horror.

"They will come for us."

Her expression hardened into a mask of cold resolve. "I know."

"We cannot remain here."

"Nothing can." She looked at her men. "Set fire to the keep."

"My lady." Jack rushed forward, his voice low. "Are you certain?"

"Burn it all."

Guy said nothing as he took her in his arms. Her men put torches to anything that would burn. Panic filled the air as smoke climbed high into the sky. De Bough's people barely escaped on stolen horses.

In the chaos of the ensuing inferno, no one took note as the five of them escaped in the darkness. Nix led the way, bearing two riders to a small cottage hidden in the forest, to freedom.

Chapter Twenty-Five

What have I done? The question repeated, over and over, in her mind.

In the cradle of his embrace, Marian leaned into Guy's strength. The horse swayed beneath them as he urged the beast through the forest, away from the inferno blazing in the distance. Her gaze drifted to the bright flames licking the sky. Dark plumes of smoke billowed around it, curling into the night in thick tendrils before disappearing.

Am I a monster? Her horrific actions haunted her. Seeing Guy and her men on their knees, at Graham's mercy, had nearly driven her mad with rage. But it had been Anne's betrayal that left her gutted and burning with fury. After all their years together, all the time spent in each other's company…she had believed them friends. Practically welcomed the maid into her home as family.

And yet she had done *his* bidding. Anne had killed her father.

Sobs choked her, and she buried her face in Guy's bloody tunic to hide her shameful tears. She mourned for them. All of them. For those she believed to be her friends, her allies. They stole everything from her for their own selfish gains. And yet, she still mourned the loss. The betrayal.

Her heart lay shattered in the smoldering ruins. Mistress Marian Ravenwood of Ravinell could no longer survive. Nothing of her remained.

Guy held her tight as they rode on, keeping her close to him. Behind them, her men followed with the remaining horses. No one spoke. They blended into the darkness, snaking their way through the forest, keeping to small paths instead of the main road. There could be no sight of them leaving Lord de Bough's holdings.

For any who had witnessed their arrival would also witness their deaths in the flames.

When they reached the cottage, Jack took care of the horses as Guy took Marian in his arms and carried her into their refuge. Inside, the men set to work, building a fire and assessing wounds. Their concerned gazes drifted to her, but Guy sheltered her in his embrace, sitting against the far wall, away from the others.

"What have I done?" The question finally breached her lips on a whisper.

Guy pressed a kiss to her temple and leaned back to meet her gaze. "You did what needed to be done."

"I killed him." The finality of the words lanced a dagger through her heart.

"You saved yourself."

"Anne is dead."

"She chose her fate."

"What of all those people in the keep? The fire?"

"They will find a way to survive. We all will." He cupped her cheek.

"I should have…"

"What is done cannot be undone." Guy's firm tone silenced the doubt in her soul.

"They will believe us dead."

"Aye." His gaze softened. "Mistress Marian Ravenwood and Sir Guy Silverthorne died in that fire."

"As traitors to the crown."

"There is none to attest to that." Guy smoothed his thumb along her jaw. "There may be rumors, but no one can reveal the truth of what transpired."

"There is nothing here for me now." Sorrow enveloped her at the thought. "Where shall we go? What shall we do?"

"We shall leave. Meradin lies to the west." He smiled and hope sprang deep within her. "We can start anew, just the two of us."

Only her men knew of their survival. If they spread the word, planted seeds telling the tale of Marian and Guy's demise at the hands of Graham de Bough, perhaps there was a chance.

They would forfeit their history, their titles, their lands, everything they had ever known in order to seize this opportunity for freedom, and it would grant them redemption. A new beginning.

Marian nodded and the darkness surrounding her mind and soul slowly faded into shadow. "I shall follow you to the ends of the earth."

Guy captured her lips in a tender kiss. Relief poured through her. She had almost lost him. Wrapping her arms around his neck, she clung to him, fearing he might be torn from her once more.

He consumed her, body and soul, completing her in ways she had never imagined. Through her pain and grief, he stood beside her, steady as an ancient oak. His lips worshipped her, and she melted into him. Two souls, bound by passion and turmoil, born anew.

Someone cleared his throat behind them. Guy broke the kiss and glared at Jack, who seemed almost abashed to interrupt their tender moment.

"I beg your pardon," he said, averting his gaze. "But will you be staying?"

Guy turned to Marian. "Can you ride?"

"Aye." She stood and faced her men. "My thanks for all you have done for me. I shall remember you fondly. Be sure to tell all you meet of our conflict with Lord de Bough, of his betrayal, of our deaths."

"We shall spread the word far and wide," John said. "All will hear of your bravery, my lady."

She embraced each of them in tearful farewell while Guy slipped from the cottage.

When she stepped into the summer night, she inhaled deeply to steady herself and to take root in her decision, to fully accept this choice to flee. The scent of smoke lingered on the breeze. She closed the door and found Guy waiting against a nearby tree. His stallion pawed impatiently beside him. Beside the black beast stood her docile gelding.

"Are you certain?" he asked, handing her the horse's reins.

"Aye."

He stepped forward and helped her mount. Then he pulled himself into his saddle. "Come, vixen, a new day awaits."

She smiled, shaking her head, and followed him deeper into darkness, knowing the bright light of a new dawn would greet them at the end of their journey.

Epilogue

Twelve Years Later, Meradin

Smoke billowed on the horizon. Guy drew his gelding to a halt and adjusted the sack slung across his back containing the provisions Marian had requested from the village. *What in the devil?* There was naught but open road between the village and Skye Lake.

Since they'd fled England all those years ago, they had remained on the outskirts of society. In Meradin, they found a haven, a refuge. In their small cottage and with some herbal skills, Marian blossomed. Guy laid down his sword and focused his efforts instead upon hunting and carpentry. Together, they carved out a piece of the countryside for themselves and remained out of sight. No one knew of their pasts, and none inquired. 'Twas paradise.

Even though Guy was content with his lot, he longed for children. Much to his dismay, he and Marian had tried to conceive. But after a few years, they accepted the truth. There would be no children from their union.

Slowly, they integrated into the village, offering their services and opening their minds. 'Twas only in the past few years, they felt comfortable venturing into the village to join local festivities. The people of Meradin welcomed them.

Early that morning, Guy ventured to town, eager to gather the last few items Marian needed to bottle mead in preparation for an upcoming festival. The king and queen of Meradin were celebrating the return of their eldest son at the autumn solstice. All the kingdom would join the celebration, even if they did not journey to the capital of Culver.

As he neared the growing plume of smoke, the scent of burning flesh and charred wood surrounded him. He nudged his horse into a canter, fear growing in the pit of his stomach.

He rounded a bend and drew to a halt at the blood-soaked horror before him. Flashes of his own past rose to haunt him as he stepped through the wreckage.

Horses lay slaughtered along the road. Mangled bodies garbed in fine livery littered the ground. Charred remains of a carriage smoldered in a heap in the ditch, as though it had been overturned and set alight. Everywhere he looked, the ruined remains of what must have been a nobleman's caravan surrounded him.

Springing from his horse, he searched the wreckage for survivors. After a while, he lost hope. There were none. Not a soul survived this massacre.

Then he saw the tiny, mangled body of a young girl, the bloody remnants of her face nearly unrecognizable. Guy doubled over, spilling the contents of his stomach onto the ground. He had seen horror in his time, but this…this was inhumane. Evil. Whoever had done this no longer possessed a soul or a conscience.

His horse whickered, drawing his attention across the expanse of horror.

A body twitched, an arm shifting in the grass.

Guy darted forward, hope taking flight in his chest. When he reached the fallen man, he dropped to his knees, searching for any sign of life. A gash split the man's chest, his cloak billowing beneath him like a blanket. Vacant eyes stared at the blue sky.

Guy rocked back on his heels. Perhaps he had imagined the motion. His heart sank again to the pit of his stomach.

The man's arm twitched, but this time, the movement came from beneath the cloak. Guy peeled back the fabric, and a pair of green eyes blinked up at him.

A sob of joy choked him. He rolled the man away and found a small girl hidden in the ditch beneath the fallen man. She stared at him, her eyes wide and fearful.

"All is well, child." He offered his hand. "Are you hurt?"

She stared at him a long moment and shook her head, not

taking his hand, her auburn curls caked with dirt and blood.

"Do you have a name?"

The girl merely blinked at him.

"You can call me Guy." He glimpsed a gold chain around her neck and a small round pendant. Whoever she was, she was no peasant's daughter. They could not tarry. Whoever had attacked could return at any moment. He needed to get her to safety.

"Would you like something to eat?"

She nodded furiously and climbed out of the ditch, throwing herself into his arms.

He cradled her against his chest and returned to his patient horse. As soon as they were astride, he kicked the horse into a run, leaving the bloody, smoldering wreckage behind.

The small girl clung to him as they rode. She buried her face in his chest and held tight. He prayed she was uninjured, as he had not checked before they fled.

Marian stood outside the cottage when it came into view. Her eyes flew wide at the sight of the bundle in his arms.

"What has happened?" She took the reins and held the horse as they dismounted.

"I found her." Guy carried the girl into the house.

Marian followed him after tethering the horse. "Where?"

Guy set the child on the edge of the bed and turned. "On the road." He launched into the tale, describing the horror of the scene and the state in which he had found the poor trembling child.

As he spoke, Marian knelt beside the child, who watched her with unflinching curiosity, and examined her for injuries. When he fell silent, she turned to the girl.

"Do you have a name?" she asked.

The little girl shook her head.

"My name is Marian, and this is my husband, Guy." She smiled kindly. "You must be hungry?"

Marian crossed the room and retrieved a small bowl of stew from the pot hanging over the fire. She placed it on the table and motioned for the girl to come sit.

The child barely came up to his waist, but she moved with speed and grace, darting to the chair where Marian waited. She snatched up the wooden spoon and shoveled vegetables into her mouth, barely chewing before stuffing more in. Her cheeks puffed up, full to bursting.

"This is lovely." Marian touched the edge of the chain around the girl's neck. "May I see it?"

The girl nodded and took another mouthful of stew.

Guy waited, watching Marian inspect the gold locket. She opened it, and her eyes flew to his. She cleared her throat and closed it, letting the girl finish her meal.

"We shall return in a moment. There is some bread on the table." Marian took his arm and steered him to the door. Once outside, she closed it behind her.

"What is it?"

"Do you have any idea who she is?" Marian kept her voice low.

"The daughter of a lord," he surmised with a shrug.

Marian shook her head, lifting her eyes toward heaven for a moment before facing him and showing him the contents of the pendant. "She is much more than that."

"What?" He ran a hand over his face. "What is she doing in the middle of a massacre?"

"Who knows? A raid turned slaughter?" She pinched the bridge of her nose. "What should we do? Shall we take her to Culver?"

"Not until I am certain of her safety."

"We cannot keep her. She is not a stray dog," Marian hissed. "Nor an orphan without family."

"God's blood, teeth, and bones." He blew out a breath as a hundred thoughts assailed him.

Marian peered through the door and a sad smile curved her lips. "Perhaps she can stay until the solstice, then we can travel to Culver. Surely, someone will be searching for her."

Guy relaxed against the doorframe, finally able to breathe again. "She will need a name."

"Ruby," Marian said, her voice soft. "For she is a rare gem."

Guy drew his wife to him, burying his face in her neck and kissing the soft skin there. "She is a treasure. A gift from heaven."

Marian leaned against him, her eyes filling with tears.

Whatever horrors they had endured, they would thrive in this aftermath. Guy and Marian would not allow this poor child to be caught in the chaos. She would survive and thrive just as they had.

This was their mission, their purpose. All roads had led them here, to this moment.

Together, they would find redemption in loving a girl named Ruby.

The End

Hello again,

Thank you so much for reading this book. If you enjoyed it, even a little, would you do me a huge favor? Please take a few minutes and write a review, and if you know someone who would enjoy this book, send them a little note and tell them about it.

If you're intimidated by writing a review, here's a blog post I wrote a few years ago to help readers formulate a helpful review: **https://kirstensblacketer.com/2018/01/11/how-to-write-a-helpful-review/**

An honest review is like a love letter to the author. It helps us grow and lets us know our hard work is appreciated. Though it may seem simple and insignificant, it means the world to hear your thoughts. Thank you for taking the time to show your love.

Also, if you'd like to be the first to know when I have a new release or get some sneak peeks into my current WIPs, then sign up for my monthly newsletter. When you subscribe, you'll get a free steamy historical short story. You can only get it as a loyal subscriber to my newsletter. I'll be offering other special short stories and giveaways as well. You won't want to miss it. You can find the sign up form on my website:

https://kirstensblacketer.com

Thank you again for your love and support! I look forward to chatting with you soon.

Sincerely,

Jen Bradlee/Kirsten S. Blacketer

ABOUT THE AUTHOR

Jen Bradlee is the alter ego of author Kirsten S. Blacketer.

Jen Bradlee can get away with murder, metaphorically speaking of course. She enjoys people watching, belly dancing, and taking walks in the rain. Give her a man who isn't afraid to get his hands dirty and plays hard. The ones with rough edges and a little scruff are the best. Comes with a warning label. "Too hot to handle."

Inspired by Tom Hiddleston and Benedict Cumberbatch, she creates characters who have multiple facets to them. The gentleman in the streets but with a wild, dangerous side behind closed doors. She loves villains and anti-heroes, bad boys and irredeemable men. We all have a dark side. Sometimes it must be freed.

http://kirstensblacketer.com/jen-bradlee

www.ingramcontent.com/pod-product-compliance
Lightning Source LLC
Chambersburg PA
CBHW061350310726
48974CB00001B/278